The One We Forgot to Love

Sandy Totten

Published in Canada
Paperback ISBN: 978-1-927625-76-7
eBook ISBN: 978-1-927625-77-4
Hardcover ISBN: 978-1-927625-78-1

Editing, Cover and Interior Design: Quarter Castle
Publishing (quartercastlepublishing.com)

About the Author

Sandy Totten was born in Middle Musquodoboit, a beautiful valley in Nova Scotia, and sings the word Musquodoboit every time she spells it, taking her back to her high school team sport days.

Growing up, Sandy lived in many different communities thanks to her dad being a carpenter, building and selling their homes, and she would continue to do so after she married her husband Dave, who also was a carpenter by trade. After having three children, she convinced her husband to settle down and has resided in Belnan for the past seventeen years where she loves tending to her vegetable garden.

Her love for books was discovered when she picked up a copy of *Anne of Green Gables* on a trip to PEI when she was ten years old, and she has been an avid reader ever since. She loves getting lost in a story and has burnt many suppers because of this. Sandy always dreamed of publishing her own stories someday and decided to take a leap of faith and share a story that she hopes resonates with readers.

Dedication

To my friend Glenda Goodyear who told me my story was worth sharing and supported my leap into this journey. Your encouragement was kind, honest, and you have only ever wanted me to succeed. Thank you for being a part of this.

To my friend Mindy George who shares my love for writing and was my support system through the entire process. From reading the entire manuscript to helping me find an editor and helping me with a satisfying ending, you will always have a special place in my heart.

To Diane, my editor and publisher, your knowledge has transformed my writing into something I can be proud of. You were patient while I asked many questions, efficient and taught me more in a few months than I had ever known. You helped my dream become a reality.

To mom and dad, thank you for supporting me my whole life and for reading this story, even the romantic parts. I love you guys.

To anyone who knows someone or who struggles with mental health, this story is for you. Please know that in dark times when you feel like you are lost and alone, there is always someone who loves you and wants to help. Never be afraid to reach out. Never be ashamed to share your story. And asking for help is a sign of strength, not weakness.

Last, but certainly not least, I dedicate this to my family. We have faced our own mental health struggles and became a stronger family because of them. While most of this story is fictional, thank you for allowing me to share parts of our life.

Dave, my love, you have my heart and always will.

Zachary, my son, your kind heart makes our family whole.

Cassidy, my daughter, your strength and perseverance is remarkable.

Abigail, my daughter, your humour is the glue that holds us together.

The One We Forgot to Love

Prologue

Adalynn

I had big dreams when I was a little girl. I was going to become an Olympic athlete (didn't matter in what sport; I loved them all), run for prime minister to solve world problems, write best-selling novels, grow the world's biggest pumpkin, marry the man of my dreams and raise children who would fill my heart with so much joy, I would literally bust. I hadn't envisioned anything other than happiness. When you are little and have parents who are hard working, kind and loyal like mine were, you simply don't think or realize life can get as hard as it does. They sheltered me as best as they could from all the bad things life inevitably threw at me. My parents created a bubble for me, and I lived in that bubble for many blissful years. I was unaware that someday, my bubble wasn't just going to pop, it was going to explode into a thousand pieces.

As a teenager, I had lots of friends in school, loved sports and had good grades. I didn't fret about anything other than what I should wear. It was back in the day before internet, when human contact was as important as the air we breathed. There were no internet bullies or social media influences on us growing up, so the drama was kept to a bare minimum. Good old-fashioned face to face communication made for lots of laughs and fond memories. Every day there was something new to do, someone to hang with, places to go. Whether it was a game of ball at the community hall, a hay loft adventure on my friend's farm, a party in someone's field or attending school dances with the best music the 80s had to offer, life was mine for the taking.

When it came time to graduate, my plans shifted a bit from becoming prime minister to finding myself and understanding what would bring me happiness for the rest of my days. I had a deep-rooted faith in God by this time and believed in the sanctity of marriage. I knew I wanted to be someone's wife and someone's mother more than I wanted to be anything else. I had so much love to offer, and I wanted that to be my number one priority in my lifetime. I still had passions I wanted to follow, but I didn't see anything on this earth being as important as loving someone else. I wanted to find a man whose passions were clear and wanted a family as much as I did.

So, when I met Dexter Cole Bartley, I knew he was the one for me. I met him at the arena in my hometown. He was coaching my cousin's hockey team and when I saw him on the bench doling out his wisdom, I felt an instant pull to him. He was sexy as all get out. Standing on top of the bench, all six feet of him, he was in total command of his surroundings. It was obvious he was in his element and had a passion to teach children a sport he clearly loved. I heard the passion in his voice. His face radiated joy, and I found myself watching him and not the game.

I wish I could say he felt the same for me when we first met, but he sort of brushed me off when I tried to introduce myself a few games later. I had waited in the rink's lobby to talk to my cousin, Layton, hoping for the opportunity to meet Dexter. I timed it perfectly and "bumped" into him as he walked by. I apologized but before I could introduce myself, he mumbled a brief "that's okay" and kept on trucking by me. Mission... unaccomplished.

Not one to be discouraged, I made myself visible whenever we met at the rink. It took a bit, but my persistence paid off when he recognized me outside the arena. He struck up a conversation with me at the grocery store, of all places. I told him I didn't think he went anywhere other than the rink, and I got my first genuine smile out of him.

His smile melted me. Looking into his dark brown eyes, I knew I was in love for sure. He told me I was a very dedicated cousin to support Layton as much as I had been. I didn't want to tell him that I was there to see him as much if not more than Layton, so I took the compliment and kept my real motive to myself. I felt divulging I was a smitten kitten at this juncture would have scared him off.

After a few more conversations at the rink over a span of a few weeks, we realized just how much we had in common. We both loved sports and had the same passion for things we loved to do. It showed in how we spoke of those things. We had the same taste in TV shows and movies, liked the same restaurants, had faith in a higher power and best of all, we enjoyed each other's company immensely.

We wasted no time in deciding we had met our match in each other and a year to the day I saw him at the rink for the first time, we were married. People talk about adjusting to married life, but I loved every single aspect of it. The part of marriage I cherished the most was waking up and starting my day with Dex beside me. There was immense comfort in knowing that someone loved me unconditionally, as flawed as I may be. I knew Dex felt the same. He knew I would be there for him through thick and thin. We got each other, too, which was a rare gift in this world. When I cried, he knew I needed to be held. If he was mad, I let him rant, and then I made him laugh. We communicated without talking, and there is a profound joy in that kind of love.

When I didn't know what career path I wanted to choose, he was patient and helped me expand my passion as a gardener. I decided to open a small shop on our 40-acre property we had bought six months into our marriage. Dexter was a carpenter with his own budding company, and he was excited to help put my passions to good use as well. He took my dreams and made it a reality, and with his craftsmanship building me the roadside veggie stand I had envisioned.

Another wonderful perk to our marriage was making love to Dex. There was nothing quite like making love to someone who loves you as much as you love them. There really was no comparison. I had slept with other guys before, and I would be lying if I said I hadn't enjoyed it, but there was an emotional connection with Dex that took sex to a whole new level. For the first five years we were married, we couldn't get enough of each other. At times, it felt like our own 50 shades. He had the power to touch my soul with one look. He made me feel sexy and taught me how to tap into the sensual side of myself. All I had to do was bite my lower lip, bat my baby blue eyes and he was ready to do whatever I wanted. We made love as often as we had wild, unadulterated sex, and I loved both equally.

Hard times did arise in our marriage from time to time, and the rose-coloured glassed I had adorned as a child had fallen off, but life with Dexter was as fulfilling as I had dreamed it could be. We loved hard, fought hard and made up hard. Whatever we did, we did together, just as I had always believed was possible.

The dream continued as we welcomed our two babies into the world five years into our marriage. Seraphina Hope was born on a cold winter's day in December and to our surprise, one week shy of a year later, Ivy Joy completed our family. Parenthood didn't dampen our love for one another. It cemented our place in each other's lives forever, and we began the next chapter in our story.

We had our hands full the first few years of being parents. With two babies so close in age, there were many, many sleepless nights. The girls were as different as night and day from the beginning. Seri slept through the night only a few short weeks into her little life, while Ivy was diagnosed with colic and cried every day for the first five months.

When they hit their respective "first" milestones, it was obvious Seri was more reserved and put more thought into each and every little thing she did. She would look her food over before putting it into her mouth, taking small bites to taste its flavour.

When she took her first steps at the tender age of twelve months, it was as if she was calculating the distance from point A to point B. She looked around to see what would hold her up if she was to fall.

Ivy, on the other hand, hadn't a care in the world. She put anything into her mouth. It didn't have to be food. Whatever she got her cute, chubby little fingers on that fit into her mouth, she started chewing on. Ivy hadn't crawled ever. She sat in the same spot on the floor and simply waited to be picked up and moved. For a little while, Dex and I thought maybe something was wrong with her motor skills, but it became apparent Ivy was simply in no hurry to do anything. She did things at her own pace, on her own time. It wasn't until she was almost two, and she was sitting on the living room floor and her grandmother came to visit that Ivy stood and took her first wobbly steps into the outstretched arms of her nana.

When the girls began to walk and talk, I didn't think my heart could handle the pure joy that coursed through it. Those two little beauties were made from love and immensely loved as well. No matter what kind of day we had or how tough things got, all the girls had to do was laugh or snuggle into Dex and me, and we felt all was right in our world.

Weeks turned into months, and months faded into years. It wasn't easy tending to two little people, keeping two businesses afloat and maintaining a good relationship with each other, but being parents had strengthened our bond for one another. It helped that we both had a good sense of humour too. Dex made the bad situations, long nights and hair-pulling moments more bearable with goofy "dad" jokes. He was serious for the most part, so when he attempted to make me laugh, it usually worked. He was no Kevin Hart, so it made a tough day easier knowing he wanted to make me laugh.

Yes, life had been very kind to me. I had nothing to complain about. It wasn't until Seri's first day of school that I saw the first signs of something that unsettled me. What that something was exactly, I couldn't put my finger on, but it nagged at me. Not enough to dwell on, but I did take notice. Seri always seemed lost in thought. Almost as if she had an imaginary friend she didn't want to tell us about. I caught her talking to herself at times and although I couldn't hear what she was muttering, it seemed to put her in a sad or bad mood more often than not.

From an early age, I knew something was different with her thought process and how she saw the world. She seemed to have the weight of the world on her shoulders and was constantly worried about germs, failing at things she tried and disappointing people. Seri was also a girl who had certain routines she couldn't stray from. If we tried to get her to change her patterns, she broke down. Saying good night to us three times was a must. If she bought one pack of gum, she had to buy all the flavours of that same brand, or she wouldn't settle leaving the store. It wasn't greed driving her (it was her allowance she was spending), but she felt incomplete if the gum wasn't a complete set. Her sweaters were always hung neatly in her closet, lined up by colours right down to their shades. She had a real fear of public bathrooms and wouldn't swim in public pools. She would not go anywhere near raw meat. Unless she watched me clean the counters to ensure nothing was cross contaminated, she wouldn't eat supper.

I should have picked up on some of those things. I really should have, but I always thought they were her idiosyncrasies. The things that made her unique. She didn't mind letting the dog lick her ice cream cone or throwing dirty clothes on the floor, so I assumed it was just certain quirks she had and nothing serious to look into.

It wasn't until her hands wouldn't stop bleeding and the skin constantly cracking open at the age of twelve that I decided to take her to a doctor. I was disturbed by what the doctor had asked me. Dr. Coldbrooke wasn't convinced Seri had chronic dry skin or any type of skin condition for that matter. He believed she was trying to scrub the germs off of her hands so hard and so often, she was destroying her skin. He asked me if she was an anxious or nervous child, and I was insulted by the question. Of course, she wasn't anxious, I told him that day. She had nothing to be anxious about. She had two loving parents who doted on her and a sister who looked up to her.

He asked Seri and I if it would be okay to set up an appointment with a psychologist to talk to Seri. I was completely blindsided at that moment and a bit angry too. I didn't see the connection between dry hands and the need to see a therapist. The stigma running rampant in my own mind I attached to mental health was a bit unnerving. The intolerance I felt at that moment was not a feeling I was proud of. Nonetheless, that was how I felt and him questioning my parenting didn't sit well with me. I curtly asked for the steroid cream for her hands. I told him that if the cream didn't work, we would be back to discuss things further.

Dexter had laughed the whole appointment off. He said that was how shrinks and doctors made their money, by getting referrals from each other. "In cahoots" were his exact words. He said Seri had lived in a loving home all her life and that if she was struggling, she would have mentioned something to us in the dozen years she had been alive.

I felt more at ease and after we sat Seri down to talk to her, she told us there was nothing for us to worry about. I felt she may have been holding something back, but she hugged me tightly and told me not to worry.

A few weeks later, the cream had worked its magic, and Seri's hands were as soft as the first time she had laid her hand in mine. Something still nagged at my heart, but I passed it off as being the over emotional human being I was and set out to make an even happier home for my family. Over the next five years, I felt I had done just that.

Had I known then what I knew now, I would have taken that appointment with the psychologist. I would have understood the gravity of the situation we were facing. I would have trusted my gut instead of worrying about what others may have thought of me as a parent. I would have put my pride aside. If I had, perhaps the agony resulting from the choice I had made that day in the doctor's office could have been avoided. Perhaps the family I had dreamed of having my whole life, the family that Dex and I had created from our love, could have weathered the storm that destroyed us.

September 17th, 2017

Seraphina

I woke ahead of my alarm. I reached up to the ledge above my captain's bed and shut it off before it made a sound. Thoughts already flew around my head faster than I could process. Today was going to be a tough day, and tears stung the back of my eyes. Hockey tryouts started in a few hours, and there was no way my parents were going to let me skip them. My parents knew how I felt about the sport. I loved hockey. The rink was my second home. I had been going to the rink since I was knee-high to a grasshopper. Only ten minutes from home, every winter, we headed to the arena five times a week, hitting the local coffee shop on the way. My entire family spent as many hours at the rink as we could. Whether it was taking part in family skates, watching Dad coach or running our hockey school, we couldn't get enough of the sport. Dad had been a rink rat his whole life, and his passion for the game ran through my blood. He was thrilled when Ivy and I decided to play hockey and with each passing hour on the ice, I was hooked.

However, today was the first time I was trying out for a team Dad wasn't a part of, in another rink with another association, and it had my stomach in knots. I had always played in my hometown with Dad at the helm and Mom a part of the team in some way. Today would be an entirely new experience for me. These facts would not escape my over-active brain. It would wake The Voice in my head, and I didn't have much strength left to deal with her...

I was five years old the first time I remember hearing the strange voice that lived in my head. It sounded like me, same pitch, same honey tone but was barely more than a whisper when it first spoke to me.

It happened on my first day of school. I had been so nervous to go but also excited to see what this big new world had to offer me. I loved being at home with Mom and my sister, but I was becoming a big girl and needed to show momma bear how brave I was and what I could do on my own. She was always proud of each of my little accomplishments, and I wanted to show her I could grow up and be my own person. Do my own things. Ivy was coming to school behind me the following year, and I wanted to have a detailed plan to lay out for her so she wouldn't be as nervous as I was as I ventured out into this new school. With no set agenda, I was determined to be brave.

I had butterflies in my belly that first day I approached the bus. I loved my purple Dora backpack I was sporting. It was full of school treasures we had gotten the week before at Staples. The striped dress I wore had every shade of pink you could think of and made me feel like such a big girl. Just like my mom when she wore dresses for special and important occasions. I felt the way Dora must have felt when she went exploring every Saturday. I would sit glued to the TV watching as her adventures unfolded. It gave me confidence knowing Dora loved every single adventure she went on, so I couldn't wait to see what excitement was in store for me at my new school.

The bus stopped on the opposite side of the street, and Mom took me by the hand, reminding me to look both ways even though the big red stop sign was sticking out to warn cars I was about to cross. She had drilled into my head there was never such a thing as being too careful.

As we got to the bus door, I was greeted by a lady I had never seen before. The butterflies in my belly moved faster. I gripped Mom's hand tighter. Think brave; be brave. I said that in my mind a few times and was half terrified and half surprised to hear a response.

"You don't need to be brave. You need to stay home where you'll be safe. It's dangerous out there."

Who had said that? And why had it sounded exactly like me? I looked up at Mom to see if maybe it had been her, but she was chatting to the bus driver. Still determined to be a big girl, I unfolded my hand from Mom's and gripped the bus railing with all my might.

I've got this. No sooner had I thought that, then another reply came.

"You aren't ready, Seri. Stay home. The world is full of scary things."

I paused on the second step. Froze is a better and more accurate description of that moment. I was sure the voice had come from me. But why was it talking to me, and who was it? Was school a scary place?

"Mommy, I don't think I want to go."

The memory was as vivid twelve years later as the day I had lived it. Fear crept up my spine that day, and my feet simply wouldn't move. I was cemented to the bottom stair of the first bus I had ever stepped on. I don't remember much else from that day or how Mom convinced me to go to school, but I remembered feeling a sense of dread. A creepy feeling that I wasn't alone, and it wasn't a friend who was keeping me company. I called this hallucination, this echo in my mind, The Voice. Not exactly an original name, but that was exactly what it was. A voice in my head. I couldn't shake the feeling of fear that I was different.

The second day of school, The Voice was back, a bit louder, bolder and definitely a lot more persistent.

"Don't go back to school, Seri. Stay with your mom. The kids don't want you there, and there are so many germs."

I wanted to run away, but where could I go to get away from myself? It didn't make sense to me. I was too little to process all that was going on and frankly, I still don't at seventeen. The Voice had only gotten more persistent and cruel as the years passed.

I had no idea how to tell my parents someone was talking to me when I was five. Nor did I now at seventeen. How did I explain to them I couldn't see who filled my head with these words but how The Voice sounded eerily like me? How did I explain there was a part of me I had no control over and who talked to me daily? That this entity was different from my thoughts; it was like an actual person resided in my head. From my first day of primary and all the years I had been alive, I did for them what I wished I could do for myself. I kept them safe from knowing about The Voice. I had kept them sane from worry and the terror that more often than not kept me up at night. I had kept my dirty, frightening secret. That I was crazy. That someone I couldn't see talked to me, and I was powerless to stop the never-ending barrage of self doubt and worry that was heaped on me by the menacing voice.

I almost came clean with my parents when I was twelve. By that time, The Voice had me so scared of germs, I had to wash my hands every single time I touched something new. I couldn't bear the thought of swimming in a pool where another person may have peed or hopped in without showering. I couldn't even fathom the snot falling out of their nasty nostrils into the over-bleached water. Stray hairs falling out of people's heads and bugs getting into public pools was not something I wanted to take part in. The Voice had pounded into my brain the importance of cleanliness, and I was its obedient minion. Anytime I was thrust into a situation I couldn't get out of, like having to use a public washroom, I had no choice but to scrub my hands raw to rid myself of the flesh-eating bacteria The Voice convinced me was multiplying on them at an alarming rate. I tried to hide my hands from Mom the best I could, but she noticed they were cracked and bleeding. No matter what hand cream she tried, they never healed. She took me to see our family doctor. Right away, this doctor saw what I had been hiding. He knew my secret. He asked questions that had nothing to do with my hands. The Voice told me to lie, so I wouldn't get in trouble or worse yet, laughed at and told I was crazy. When the doctor mentioned to Mom I should maybe see a therapist, the look on her face was what I had feared. Disbelief. Disgust. Shock. I almost broke free of my shame and told them what was happening but for once, The Voice was comforting at that moment.

"Don't worry, Seri. I understand you. I'll always be here. You don't need your family's pity. I am your family too. I'll take care of you." Odd how I believed that to be true. The Voice that always had my stomach in knots and fists clenched tightly, telling me I was no good was also a source of comfort. It was the most perplexing relationship I had with anyone or anything. This voice, this sweet, sharp-tongued voice had stripped me of my self-confidence and self-worth, and yet I believed it when it told me I was better off trusting it than my family. So, I stayed silent that night when Mom and Dad sat me down and asked if I had anything I wanted to tell them. I told them I washed my hands a lot, but it was more of a habit than anything else.

The relief on their faces and the absence of The Voice in my head that night led me to believe I had made the right decision.

However, as I stared up at the ceiling and wondered what I could come up with to get out of going to the tryouts today, a huge part of me wished I had confessed that night five years ago. Maybe then I would no longer have to endure the mental anguish I faced almost daily. Right on cue, The Voice began its slow and steady relentless nagging.

"You could always break a bone. Can't tryout in pieces."

"A bit drastic, don't you think?" I whispered. "Wouldn't an upset tummy suffice?"

"Your mom won't believe that. She'll make you go. You know what she gets like."

"Yes. I know what my mother gets like. She's my mother, not yours," I snapped back.

Mom loved me so much and pushed me hard to do what she thought I was capable of, what she knew would make me happy even if it took me a bit longer to see that. What she didn't get was at times, her pushing almost drove me past the point of my own sanity. The Voice and my mother had two very different views of how my life should be and the more she pushed me, the louder The Voice became. It was obvious to Mom that I struggled, but she didn't know with what exactly, and I didn't know how to tell her. I desperately wanted to share with her all I had been through. How my mind worked and the terror that gripped me. But she wouldn't understand. She would be frightened for and of me. She would think less of me and think I was crazy. She wouldn't love me the same. I knew she wouldn't because I loathed myself for being this way. Most days lately, I hated myself. I couldn't stand the thought of Mom looking at me the way I did when I stood in front of the mirror. I didn't think I would survive if she looked at me the way I looked at myself.

If I shared with anyone what was happening in my head, that would only make The Voice louder. The Voice warned me many times that I would be laughed at if I tried to explain my situation and that I would place a heavy burden on those I loved.

Reluctantly, I put up with Mom's constant presence in my space and her incessant fretting without telling her my real issue. I couldn't imagine what Dad might say about the whole thing. He would likely ground me for a few months and tell me I was crazy. He loved me, but he had no patience for things he didn't understand. Since I didn't understand what I was going through, I was determined not to burden my family with The Voice that controlled my life.

Reluctantly, I rose, changed into my workout gear and threw on my headphones. I cranked the tunes to silence the unwanted conversation I was having with myself. Out in the hall, I ran into Ivy. I pulled one earpiece out to hear what she was saying.

"Hey, Seri, excited for tryouts?"

Ivy and I were only a year apart in age, so every second year we got to be teammates. This was the year. Mom and Dad loved it because we headed in the same direction all winter instead of splitting up.

"I guess so. Not sure I'll make it though." At that moment, I wished I was Ivy with no worries and no voice looming in my mind. She annoyed me because she had no idea how lucky she was.

"That should be me saying that. You're the shoe in. I'll be lucky to get selected to carry water bottles," Ivy said, chuckling.

She was a fantastic player but played more for the social aspect of the game than the competitive side. She didn't care what level she played. On the other hand, I ate, slept and breathed hockey. I loved the sound skate blades made on ice as they sliced through its thickness. The way I balanced on one skate almost parallel to the ice surface on a tight turn. The feeling of the puck lifting off the ice and going top shelf past the goalie. I was the leading scorer last year. I stood a good chance at making this team if I believed in myself...

"You won't make it!" The Voice violently sliced through my mind, ripping the good thoughts to shreds. "Stop getting so excited, Seri... It'll only make you feel miserable when you get cut. Daddy was the coach last year. That's why you made it."

I didn't want to talk about tryouts anymore, so I ignored Ivy, who was still talking, and headed downstairs to get my gear ready. I opened the stand-up equipment bag and breathed a sigh of relief seeing each piece of gear in its exact spot. One less worry for the day. The Voice must have been okay with it too because it stayed silent. One time mine and Ivy's bags had gotten mixed up, and I had a complete meltdown at the rink. Our gear bags were identical on the outside but when I went to open the bag, I smelt Ivy's gear before I saw it. Upon opening the bag, the disorder of the whole thing had sent me over the edge. I remembered being hysterical and making a huge scene in the dressing room. Mom had to physically remove me from the room, and the awkward stares from teammates in the weeks following my outburst hurt my heart. They thought me childish for acting like that, but the chaos of the gear bag was too much for The Voice, who had been raging in my head, and it had pushed me over the edge.

I closed the bag and started for the stairs.

"You're wasting your time. Why put yourself through this, Seri? You will only fail. And we both know how much you hate to fail." My steps slowed. I did hate failure, and my thoughts began to match The Voice's reasoning.

"That's it, Seri. You are seeing the light. You saw the list of names trying out. How do you expect to compete with those girls?"

Giving space for these thoughts to grow, I began to believe what I was hearing. I had seen the list. Every girl except for two or three could make the team easily. Panic closed in on me. If I was going to get out of this, I needed to do something soon.

"Why not take a little spill down the stairs? There are only five of them, so you won't die but hopefully break a bone. You can tell your parents you tripped."

The ridiculous idea germinated and took root. I wouldn't have to break any bones. A few bruises may do the trick. It would have to be a loud thump so they knew I had fallen.

"I don't want to break anything. I'll hope for a bad bruise."

I climbed the stairs. Part of me was shocked I was going this far, but The Voice was soothing and kind now. "It'll be okay, Seri. You'll be much happier at home once this part is over. You're happiest at home."

I felt like I was in a fog. I reached the top of the stairs. "I don't know about this."

I didn't feel like the choice was mine anymore. I was going to follow through with The Voice's idea. If I wanted to silence the incessant nagging, this was the only solution.

"Who are you talking to?" Ivy's question broke up the conversation going on with my mind.

"What? Oh, just talking to myself. Making sure I had everything." I paused at the top of the stairs. I wondered if I could still make it look like an accident in front of Ivy. I could pretend I had forgotten something and miss a stair in my haste.

"Funny, cause I thought I heard you say if I fell down the stairs, bruises were as good as broken bones. What the hell were you talking about, ya nut? And to who?" She laughed.

Without realizing it, Ivy's words cut right to my heart. Yes, I was a nut. And I knew it. If you knew the whole of it, Ivy, you'd really laugh.

"I was singing, not talking." I stormed out the door, not able to follow through on the plan that had been hatching. "Get your gear, and let's get going. I don't want Mom on our ass." And with that, I had lost my opportunity to miss tryouts. I would have to figure out a way to drown out The Voice and get through the day.

Ivy

Did I ever love being at the rink. Any rink really. Home away from home is what our family called it. Dad had bought me skates when I was a little squirt. While I don't remember really liking the skating part, it sure was fun to have Dad carry me in his arms while he glided around the ice. Dad was a phenomenal skater. The wind turned my cheeks rosy, and I giggled from the joy of being on the ice. Seri was right behind us, chasing us down. She didn't like to be carried. As soon as she had learned to skate, that was that. She was flying. Mom stood on the sidelines taking thousands of pictures at family skates and cheering us on.

Family skates morphed into a hockey school run by my parents, and then we turned our love for skating and hockey into an entire girls' hockey team. That was rare in our area. The last girls' team had been twenty years before my time. Dad was our coach. Well, my coach every second year. He stuck with Seri's age group until this year. I wanted him to coach me the second year Seri and I were in different levels, but Seri wouldn't play without him coaching. She got pretty worked up when he told her he was going to coach me instead. I told him to stick with her after Seri's meltdown about it. I could break in another coach just fine.

The rink had always been a place where I could be myself and be accepted. My absolute favourite thing about it was the friendships I had forged over the years. I appreciated the cold crisp air that filled my lungs even when I was gasping for air during practices, wondering if I would be alive at the end of them. I revelled in the rush of excitement when I released a slap shot. I loved getting hot chocolate and beaver tails from the cafeteria and chatting with the lady behind the counter. She always asked how practice or my game was, and I always replied with, "Deadly, but I got through knowing you'd have my beavertail ready."

Today, we were on our way to tryouts in town. A first for Seri and me. We usually played on a team in our community, but this year the boundaries had changed for female hockey. We now had to travel to town to play at the higher levels. It was a bone of contention with my parents, but they knew we wanted to play, so they were taking us to town to tryout, despite how they felt.

When we pulled up to the Mac Center, I hopped out before we came to a full stop, ready and raring to go. I was excited to see the girls who would be at tryouts. Oh, and, of course, I was pumped thinking of all the oxygen I would take in as I laboured around the ice for two solid hours.

Seri and I got dropped off at the door, while Mom and Dad went to get coffee. We headed into the new arena that was nestled in the heart of Avano, a town forty minutes from home. It was all my eyes could do to take it all in. The ceiling seemed to be nestled in the sky. It was extremely high and made mostly of glass that made the clouds look like they were resting on them.

Straight ahead through automatic doors was the lobby. It was dull grey in color everywhere I looked. The walls, floors, light fixtures and doors were all grey with the exception of a brown folding table smack dab in the centre of the lobby. It was set up with two stacks of jerseys, one on each side of the table. Like a shrewd detective, I said to Seri, "This must be where we sign up and get a jersey."

Seri rolled her eyes. "No shit, Sherlock."

I glanced at her and started to reply but thought better of it. Seri hadn't spoken one word on the way into town. As we pulled into the parking lot, I noticed her bottom lip quivering. I was still trying to process what I had heard her say at home about falling down the stairs and not breaking bones just getting bruises. Had I heard her right? What was going through that mind of hers, I was never too sure.

Whatever she was thinking about now, I knew her well enough to know she was not fit to talk to at this time. She would be bitchy. She wasn't going to ruin this day for me. What did she have to worry about anyways? She was a shoe in for any team she wanted to play on. She could skate like the wind and had a work ethic that made me look completely lazy. Because she was one of the best players, the kids gravitated to her like mice to cheese. I too had lots of friends, but it was my humour not my hustle that kept my posse coming back for more. I was okay with that. Being funny wasn't as calorie burning as skating, and that suited me just fine.

There was a part of me that wasn't looking forward to tryouts with Seri this year. She was the better player, and I hated being compared to her. "Put some effort in, Ivy, like your sister." "Skate harder, Ivy. You can skate as fast as your sister." All season long, that's what I had to listen to. Not that my parents weren't right or malice when they said those things. I had oodles of potential. I could keep up to Seri when I wanted to. It was just that I played to have fun and socialize, which to me was just as important as winning. I put in enough effort to help my team win and concentrated on slapping that puck into the net with as much force as I could muster, but I wasn't going to play hockey after minor hockey. So, I wanted to play more for fun than strictly competitive reasons. I certainly didn't share that philosophy with my coach, who was also my father every other year because he was over the top competitive like Seri. He would eat me for breakfast if I shared this with him. I was not built to be a competitor. I was built for comic relief and good times. I'd leave the excellence to Seri.

The other part of me loved being Seri's teammate. When Seri was relaxed (which seemed way less often lately), she was a treat to be around. She had the best belly laugh when she chose to let loose, and it was contagious in the dressing room. She always made sure to sit by me and never let anyone say anything bad to me or about me. More than once, she went to the penalty box defending me. Even though I was almost six feet tall and she was barely a bit taller than a hobbit, she was feisty when someone even looked at me wrong. That somehow made me feel important, like I mattered to Seri. I didn't feel that way too often anymore in my family. Like I mattered. This sounded dramatic, but sometimes I felt like the one they had forgotten to love. That they thought because I was happy, I didn't need their attention. That couldn't have been further from the truth. I needed Mom and Dad as much as Seri did. Because I didn't bring the drama like Seri, didn't mean I didn't want their time. It seemed like I was an after thought now. Lately, Mom worried more and more about Seri, and I couldn't figure out why. If Seri had a problem, she wasn't a shy person. She would tell us exactly what she thought, so why was Mom always catering to her?

Seri had been aloof for as long as I could remember. When we were little, there were times when we played outside in the dirt while Mom was gardening and all of a sudden, Seri would break down into tears and tell me to stop talking. What struck me as odd was most of those times, I hadn't said a damn thing. I would get the blame though, followed by one of those looks Mom liked to shoot at me that said, "Don't get your sister going." Seri would cry about how dirty she was, and Mom would bathe her to calm her down.

When Seri wasn't a ball of worry, she was a great big sister. On and off the ice. I just wished she would take the stick out of her ass and chill out more often. She had nothing to be scared of today. She would rock the tryouts like she always did.

Seri and I signed in, and I was happy to learn we were assigned to the same team and dressing room. She asked if she could have a certain number, but I didn't care which one I got and took what they handed to me. Agitation rose in Seri when she realized they didn't have the number she wanted. She wore the same number for years, and changing it on tryout day was not going to sit good with her. The ladies behind the table exchanged looks, as if to say they were dealing with a diva, but I knew the problem was deeper than just a number. How deep, I couldn't quite figure out. I tried to lighten the mood.

"Number three; that's a hat trick! That could be a good omen. Change isn't always bad." Her look of despair was beginning to dampen my mood. I tried again. "Teammates today, Seri! Just like at home." I waited for a reply, and none came. "Okay. Good talking to ya then." I picked up my pace, and Seri fell behind. This wasn't going to be a fun experience if she didn't soon get out of her bad mood, and I didn't feel like being dragged down by her sourness no matter what was bothering her.

Opening the dressing room door, I was first assaulted by the smell of stale hockey gear that most had forgotten to air out over the summer, and then by my friend Hannah, whom I hadn't seen since our championship game last March.

"Hey, Ives!! What's shakin', bacon?" Hannah welcomed me with open arms.

"Not too much. Just here to bring the show. Whether shit or skill will soon be determined," I replied, and Hannah laughed.

"You're a character, gurl. Your slap shot is all you need to fire up, and you will have no worries. Oh, hey, Seri! Glad you are on our team today!"

I turned in time to see Seri enter the dressing room, roll her eyes and mutter, "Yeah, that's great," before shuffling past us and taking a seat in the corner. It irked me that Seri had been rude to Hannah, and I tried to cover for Seri to make her look like less of the jerk than she had been. I leaned in closer to Hannah and whispered, "She's really nervous. She gets quiet when she's this nervous."

Hannah smiled and nodded. "I get that. I have butterflies too." But when Hannah's eyes met Seri's again, Seri offered no smile in return. Hannah's smiled faded, and she didn't seem convinced by what I had said.

Wanting to move past the awkward moment, I went to where Seri had plunked herself down and began to get dressed.

"What was with the 'tude, dude? Hannah was just trying to say hi."

Seri didn't look at me. She was tightening the straps on her shin pad. "I have bigger things to worry about than saying hi to anyone. Leave me alone, okay?"

Was it just me, or did I sense an underlying tone in Seri's voice? She sounded bitchy, yet her eyes and her last sentence seemed to convey panic. I couldn't shake the feeling she wasn't talking to me.

I was a slow dresser, so I decided to focus on the task at hand, which was to get on the ice on time. Wouldn't look too sharp if I was late first day, first tryout. I had my work cut out for me as it was, and I doubted my radiant wit and whimsical humour would get me to the next round of tryouts. Not with the talent I saw in this room.

The dressing room filled quickly. Half the girls I had played against at one time or another, and the other half were girls I had played with last year. The volume of the room was a bit lower than normal at first but soon filled with laughter and stories of what the summer had entailed. Everyone was chatting. Well, everyone but Seri.

Twenty minutes flew by and just under the wire, I was as ready as I'd ever be to hit the ice and rock the tryouts.

Adalynn

itting rink side bundled in a winter jacket, my heart swelled with pride watching Seri and Ivy skate. I was definitely one of "those" hockey moms. The one people shied away from and tried not to sit beside because they never knew what was going to come out of me. I would love to say I never hollered and I was a calm fan, but I wore my emotions on my sleeve, and there were places these emotions came spouting out of me. The rink was one of those locations. There had been talk once of the girls and Dex banning me from their games. They had said I could be quite embarrassing at times and although I was appalled, more accurately, I resembled that remark. I was an overprotective mamma bear to start, so watching the girls play a sport where things got rough, I admit, at times, special occasions if you would, I got an octave higher than my indoor voice. Or, as Ivy delicately told me, "You sound part wounded animal and part demon possessed."

I argued back saying most of what I yelled was encouraging, to which she replied, "Who can tell the difference with those veins in your neck popping out and the f-bomb flying everywhere. Your face turns seven shades of red to boot." Good ole Ivy. She painted a pretty and maybe a tiny bit accurate picture of what I could turn into.

I was given strict orders to say nothing at these tryouts. This was my trial run. If I could stay quiet during these next few weeks, they would consider letting me watch them play this season. They were getting older and as teenagers, everything I did was embarrassing somehow. I planned on doing all I could to keep my word. Sit down like a well-behaved fan, but you know what they say about best laid plans. After all, it wasn't like I yelled at refs... very much. I mostly shouted words of encouragement. Things like, "Skate, Ivy! Hurry, Seri! Move your feet! Get the puck! Get in the corner! Don't take that shit!"

I chuckled to myself as I realized perhaps I was a bit over the top. That my emotions, good or bad, always bubbled up out of me. But I didn't know how else to be. I felt emotions strongly, and that was all there was to it.

Empathy was the emotion that consumed me. My entire life, I have always felt strong empathy for others. When I was in grade six, my best friend told me she was going to need extra help reading to catch up to her classmates. She needed to put extra time in at lunch and after school. I can still picture her leaning over to me and whispering, "I didn't know I was that dumb," and tears falling down her cheeks. That was the first time I remember crying for someone other than myself. I sat with her every day at lunch and sometimes stayed after school until she got a handle on reading. I couldn't leave her behind. One girl made fun of her, and I did the only thing a good friend could do at that moment. I slugged her with my lunch can. The two-week detention and ass whooping from my father was certainly worth it when I saw how happy my friend was that she wasn't facing her struggles alone.

As the years went by, I realized it was both a blessing and a curse to feel as much as I did. The little things in life brought much more joy than I expected. Ocean waves and the crackling of a fire mesmerized me for hours. A bee suckling inside a flower filled my heart with wonder. A passing moment with a good soul stayed in my memory and would until my dying day. But the painful moments took an incredible toll on my heart. If I saw someone struggling, I felt the weight of their load. A fight with a family member or friend bothered me for a long time. When my grandparents passed away, I felt like I couldn't go on.

Having children only heightened my empathy to a level that at times was completely overwhelming and suffocating. When they hurt, I hurt twice as much. If they cried, I sobbed. If they were mad, I was furious. If something made them happy, I was ecstatic for them. Like I told Seri one time, whatever they were going through, it seemed like I stole their emotional thunder. I was always riding a notch higher or lower on the feeling scale than they were. Not on purpose, let me assure you. If I had one wish to change anything about myself, it would be the depth I felt my emotions. Feeling them was great, but sometimes they sucked the life out of me. Case in point: Seri. There wasn't anyone on this earth I worried about more than my oldest daughter.

I looked down on the ice and saw Seri playing centre. The puck dropped to start the game. She won the draw back to Ivy, who was playing defence. The sound of their skates on the ice, the crisp passing between my girls, fuelled my spirit and I yelled out, "Go girls," before I could stop myself.

Ivy looked up and shook her head, but she had a smile forming behind her face shield. She was likely looking around to see where everyone was sitting. She wasn't only social off the ice. The girl kept her eye on the hockey fans while playing. When she thought it was okay to do so, she flashed them a quick smile or offered a wink or a wave during play. I couldn't help but smile back at my talented social butterfly, and I moved my hand across my mouth in a zipper fashion to let her know that was my one and only outburst. She shook her head up and down in what I would like to believe was in agreement, but I knew it was more of a mmmm hmmm action.

Seri was kicking ass and taking names. That wasn't just a proud mom talking. That was fact. She had aggression on the ice that sometimes surprised me. Her strides were powerful, and she had no qualms meeting a competitor in the corner. It was 15 minutes into the game, and she had scored once and had an assist in the 2-0 game.

I looked around to see where Dex was watching from. He wasn't keen on watching hockey with me when he wasn't coaching for the above-mentioned reasons. He didn't believe I had the capacity to stay quiet for 45 minutes. I wondered if he had heard my little outburst during the first period. I had no doubt he would tell me in the car if he had. My eyes spotted him along the boards with a few other hockey dads. It was a pleasant feeling to have all of us in the rink, enjoying all this game had to offer.

As the last minutes of the game played out, Ivy wound up and riffled a slap shot that hit the crossbar and sailed up into the air 50 feet. That girl could shoot a puck! I stood up, raised a fist in the air but caught myself before yelling out. She looked up in anticipation of me blurting something out. She giggled, and I tried not to reciprocate, just playing it cool like I was shifting in my seat.

The buzzer sounded, and I made my way to the lobby with the moms I had been sitting with to wait for my girls. Seri was the first one out, a surprise to no one. No doubt Ivy was hamming it up in the room with her friends. A tug at my heart had me wishing Seri was a bit more like Ivy. I felt guilty for the thought, but Ivy was carefree and funny. Seri was much too broody and a bit of a loner for my liking.

"How was it, Seri? Happy to be on the ice again?" I asked when she approached.

For a split second, her eyes lit up. The passion for the game evident in their sparkle. But as quickly as it had appeared, it was gone.

"It was fine, Mom. Let's not talk about it, okay?" A typical Seri response.

Deflated, I changed the subject. "Was Ivy almost ready to go?"

This question brought a smile to her face. "Oh, yeah, almost. We should see her in about a week."

Grateful the mood had been lightened, I hooked my arm around her neck, and we shuffled off to the car, leaving Ivy to find us when she was ready.

Dexter

I saw both girls in the rear-view mirror. Ivy was chatting up a storm, filling us in on how things went from the time she had gotten her jersey until she returned to the car. I was passing cars on the highway at the same rate of speed Ivy was talking, which was rather quickly. There was no chance of anyone getting a word in edgewise for at least another ten minutes. Her face was beet red, and her hair looked like she had come out of the shower. It amazed me at how effortlessly Ivy made hockey look and how smart she was on the ice. She made many plays and could see the ice like some of the great professional players. It baffled me she played more for fun than competition. She was not interested in taking hockey further and although I had come to terms with her decision, sometimes it pissed me off for her to have that kind of natural talent and not want to do something with it.

Seri was sitting quietly with her hands folded on her lap, staring out the window. She was as red as Ivy in the cheeks, but that was the only tell-tale sign she had just been on the ice. Knowing Seri, she was likely thinking of the mistakes she had made in the game. Which, from what I saw, weren't too damn many. She was a work horse on the ice. While she wasn't as naturally talented as Ivy, she made up for it tenfold with her work ethic. She loved the game. It was as obvious as the love my wife had for her garden. When Seri was little, the smile on her face was as wide as her strides on the ice. Her tongue stuck out a bit, deep in concentration as she learned to lift the puck up and over the goalie during games. Nothing filled my heart with as much pride as watching her develop into the player she worked so hard to become. As she grew, so did her love for the sport but so too did a sense of hesitancy. Addie asked her about it one time, and all Seri said was she didn't want to let anyone down. No good athlete wanted to let their teammates down, so I accepted the answer at face value. Watching her now, sitting in the backseat like she had lost her best friend, made me wonder if she was thinking that very thought. I felt myself getting mad even before asking any questions because a part of me knew Seri would say she didn't play great. Ivy paused long enough to take a breath, and I seized the opportunity.

"How do you feel it went, Seri?"

She lifted her head, and our eyes met briefly in the mirror.

"Okay, I guess."

"Why just okay? I thought you and Ivy did very well. I suspect you'll both make the first round of cuts easily."

When no response came, I found myself annoyed that she was so gloomy. To be honest, I had a hard time relating to Seri in general most days. The older she got, the harder it was for me to understand why she had no confidence and a hundred different quirks and routines that did nothing but bog her down. She didn't see it that way though. Without her little routines, she was lost. Ironically, her routines and the way they controlled her life had me feeling less in control. As the man of the family I had built with Addie, with each passing day, I was less sure of how to communicate with Seri and keep our family on track and happy.

When I was growing up, we didn't talk about feelings. Hell, I wasn't sure my father had any real emotions other than being constantly annoyed. He was a great provider, put me in every sport I wanted to play but I knew, sure as shit, if I talked about how I felt on any matter, I would have gotten a solid back hand and told I was ungrateful. That's not to say my father was unkind. That was just how it was back in those days. Feelings were not to be discussed. I remembered one time telling Dad I didn't want to finish playing hockey my final year of high school, and he looked at me and said, "Boy, you'll play, and you'll love it. I ain't raising no lazy kids or quitters." That had been the entire discussion. He hadn't asked why I wanted to quit. It hadn't mattered to him. He simply wasn't going to allow it. He saw the talent I had, and that was that. I would be finishing out my final year. That year, I broke the scoring and most penalty minutes records and had a blast doing it. Sometimes parents know better than their kids what is good for them.

Fast forward all these years later, and I found myself more like my old man than I cared to admit. Isn't that what I was doing with Ivy and Seri? I had never asked Ivy if she wanted to quit hockey, and I don't think her answer would have changed the fact I would have made her play. When it came to feelings, well, I had no interest in opening up that Pandora's box with Seri. She felt things differently than I did, and I was more than terrified I would be unequipped to deal with what she was going through if she shared her thoughts with me. That was not a failure I was going to take on as her father. Tough love had worked for me. It would work with Seri too. Seri knew I loved her and believed in her. I didn't need to tell her.

Addie and I were not of the same mind on this touchy subject. She felt I wasn't taking Seri's mental health seriously enough. Every time I turned around, she was pressing me on the issue. She fed into the notion that the more we talked about it, the better we would feel about things. I felt the more we discussed it, the further apart we became. She had this unshakeable feeling Seri needed professional help. I blamed our family doctor for bringing up that possibility. The seed of needing professional help took root in her mind and blossomed into a large hedge with us on opposite sides. We couldn't see each other's side anymore. Our marriage was slowly but surely unravelling over our different approaches with Seri. Addie felt that the older Seri got, the more her mind became lost in all her daily rituals, fear of germs, fear of people hating her and the constant need to be at home. I didn't think Addie was wrong exactly. I just thought babying Seri was not the way to solve anything and maybe even the root of the problem.

A song popped into my head. "The wheels on the bus go round and round, round and round, round and round..." That's what it felt like lately. That the wheels kept spinning, but I wasn't getting anywhere.

I pulled my thoughts back to the hockey tryouts and the girls.

"Well, I bet you both get called back." I pressed on, not really expecting a reply.

"I have the same feeling," Adalynn chimed in. She had been silent up until that point. "Seri, you did great! Did you talk to anyone in the room? Did you feel comfortable out there?"

Of course, Addie would ask a million questions, all directed at Seri. It grated my nerves that she had to dive deep into every aspect of Seri's day. How did you feel? How did you put your gear on? Did you take a piss before you started, and what colour was it? Ok, so they weren't the exact questions she was asking, but I'm sure if given enough time, she would ask them.

Seri mumbled her replies.

I tuned them out and turned up the radio. There was no reason for me to be this irritated. Addie was only trying to gauge Seri's mood, but she had yet to ask Ivy a single question. Not that Ivy noticed. She was the best natured kid I'd come across. She let everything roll off her back like a turtleback green on a golf course. I looked at Ivy in the rear-view, and she was staring at me. She winked, causing me to smile. That girl was a breath of fresh air when I felt I was drowning.

October 1st, 2017

Ivy

I was a pretty easy going girl, but tonight I found myself anxious. We were two weeks, six practices and four games into the AAA tryouts. Any minute now Mom was going to get an email that would tell Seri and me if we had made the team. I don't remember being nervous about being cut from anything, but this time I was invested. The more cuts I made it through, the more confidence I gained. I had been shocked and, to my surprise, ecstatic in the last game when I scored the game-winning goal to edge out our rivals in a pre-season tournament to head to the semis tomorrow. The tournament was designed for teams in the AAA league to pick their final rosters. To find myself still among the best in our region had me feeling pretty good about life. I wasn't used to excelling at hockey.

I had no one to blame but myself because I didn't have a long attention span and effort was low on my list of priorities at times. I liked hockey. A lot. It took serious chops to put the practice in to continuously improve though, and I would rather soak in a good YouTube "how to" channel than shoot a hundred pucks into a net. With this little taste of hard work and the reward of being considered for this team, I began to see that Mom and Dad may have been on to something when they said I had talent I hadn't decided to use. They weren't blowing smoke up my you know what. I could achieve good things if I worked hard. It was a nice feeling being down to the final eight defence. We started with twenty-two. Only two left to be cut, and I had a real shot of making it!

Seri, of course, was still there and since she was leading the team in scoring, the email tonight was more to tell me my future than hers. She would have to break both ankles and score on her own net three times at this point to be cut. She didn't seem to enjoy hockey yet. I knew it was a major adjustment for her not to have Dad coaching, but I had been sure the love for the game would have perked her up by now. I glanced at Seri, who had finished clearing the supper dishes off the table and was filling the sink with water to wash them. It was my turn to dry the dishes, so I was biding my time, sitting at the table. I twirled the dish towel around in circles with both my hands and as it wound tighter and tighter, I wondered if I should reach out and whack Seri with it. Oh man, that would be so funny and would sting like a bugger. Mom and Dad wouldn't share my kind of humour and since both were still at the table with me, I opted to keep twirling and wait for an opportune moment to pounce.

"Have you checked yet, Momsie?" I asked for the tenth time.

Mom reached for her phone sitting on the table and refreshed her email. She looked surprised this time and clicked on a message. By the way she was reading, it was the email we had been waiting for.

Dad got out of his chair and stood behind Mom. She looked up at him as he read, and I could tell the news wasn't what I had been hoping for. Dad put his hand on Mom's shoulder and shifted his gaze to me.

"Ives, I want to tell you I couldn't have been prouder of how hard you worked out there and that no matter what we tell you right now, you are AAA in our book."

Well, that's never a good pep talk. I didn't need to have it spelled out for me.

"No biggie. I made it farther than anyone thought I would." Surprisingly, a lump formed in my throat, and tears stung the corner of my eyes.

"Hey, could've went either way. You worked the hardest I've ever seen you work." Dad walked over and awkwardly rustled the top of my hair.

"Yeah, hard work got me cut on the last tryout instead of the first." I tried to laugh and lighten my mood, but my joke fell short. I didn't bother to ask if Seri was on the list because, well, let's face it; she deserved to be. She worked like a dog out there on the ice and had skill to back up her work ethic. I couldn't be mad or even jealous of her success. She was driven. Sometimes it seemed she was driven by crazy ass demons, but still she put in the work.

"Well, Mom and Dad haven't given you the sad puppy dog eyes or you are AAA no matter who cuts you speech, Seri, so I guess I should congratulate you on making the team." I looked to the sink where Seri stood. She was scrubbing the frying pan so hard, I was convinced the handle was going to snap in two.

"Seri, you okay?" The question came from Mom. Mom stood and made her way to the sink. "You did make it, Seri. You should be happy. We're so proud of you."

I stopped fiddling with the dish towel and took in the scene unfolding in front of me. Seri, the golden child, had just been told she had made the top team of the top league for our age bracket in our province and there stood Mom, stroking Seri's back, doing all she could to make this news more exciting to her ears. Yet, here I sat, feeling like I could burst into tears at any moment after getting axed in the final hour, and I was watching our mother, my mother, sooth Seri.

Dad was still standing beside me, seemingly unaware of the slight Mom had unintentionally heaped upon me. He leaned down and in a rare gesture, kissed my cheek.

"I know you don't really care where you play, Ivy, and you'll have fun in AA, but be proud of yourself, kid. You did all you could, and that's all anyone can ask of you. Next year, I have no doubt you will be a starter on the AAA team."

"Thanks, Daddio. Hey!" A cheery thought struck me. "I just realized I will be playing for you again this year. You didn't think you could get rid of me that easily, did you?" Just the thought of being on Dad's team brightened my mood tremendously. I had forgotten Dad had been asked to coach AA this year. That was a pretty good league too.

Dad started to reply, but something near the sink caught his attention. I looked over and was shocked to see Seri sobbing uncontrollably. What the hell was she going through?

"Seri, what's wrong?" I asked, cautiously starting towards her.

"I can't. I can't. I can't," Seri repeated. Each time she repeated it, she got louder and more robotic sounding. She rocked back and forth. What couldn't she do? What was going on with her? Where was this madness coming from? It was almost comical, except it frightened me. Mom was still beside Seri, rubbing her back so hard, I was surprised she didn't catch fire from the friction.

"I think you misunderstood, Seri. I got cut. You," I poked her on the nose, "are still on the team. I'm supposed to be crying."

Mom shot me one of her "you know better than that, Ivy" looks, and I stepped back. I didn't want to get caught between a mamma bear and her favourite bear cub. Heaven forbid I try to help Seri.

Dad was now at the sink too and took control of the situation. He carefully stepped in between Mom and Seri and guided Seri to a seat at the table. He pulled up a chair beside her, and Mom took up the chair on her other side. I stood a few feet back from them, unsure of what to do.

"Seri, what's gotten into you? Are you upset for Ivy?" Dad asked.

Fat chance, I thought. Seri wasn't capable of thinking of anyone most days but herself. I loved my sister, I really did, but empathy wasn't her area. It wasn't even in her postal code. I watched my sister try to take deep breaths amidst the tears, but it was hard for her. My annoyance for my mother and Seri quickly faded into genuine concern. Seri was seriously struggling, and we had yet to understand why.

"Deep breaths, Seri. That's it. Talk to us. What's wrong?" Mom's voice was calm, but her eyes held despair.

"I can't. I can't go back without Ivy." Seri talked between gulps of air. "I won't have anyone with me. Not Dad. Not Ivy. I just can't. I'll let you all down. I'm not good enough to play AAA." Fresh tears overtook her, and she crumbled into Mom's lap.

I didn't know how to process what I heard. I would kill to be in Seri's shoes, and all Seri desperately wanted to do was cut off her feet. Strange, wasn't it? How could I have lived with someone for sixteen years and not understand how their mind worked? I had no idea what could possibly be going through Seri's mind. How was she so oblivious to my feelings and the fact I was cut from the team she would be the star of? And what was worse, she had no clue she was an amazing player! I used to think she said stupid things like she would let us down or she was no good for attention, but it finally dawned on me; she was actually thinking those things. That at this moment, Seri really believed she would be terrible if she played AAA. Mind blowing information.

I took the final few steps to Seri.

"Seri?" She raised her head to look at me. I knelt down and hugged her. I held on tightly. "I love you, Seri. I'll still be there as your number one fan. I will come to every game you play and cheer like Mom does."

I got a snort out of Seri. No one wanted anyone to cheer like Mom did.

"Hey, Ivy, I resemble that remark!" Mom chimed in, and she softly laid a hand on my back. I was helping Seri, so I guess I was worth Mom's attention. I felt like an ass the second the thought entered my mind. I didn't have kids, so I had no right to judge how Mom handled Seri, and these outbursts were getting more frequent and certainly more illogical. It was no wonder she hovered over her constantly. My own heart was breaking for Seri, but another part of me, the bigger part, was getting tired of being overlooked to deal with Seri's silliness.

"Well, that's enough of this foolishness for one night." Dad stood. "I have to run to the store and get milk for breakfast. Seri, pull it together, and let's get some fresh air."

I would love to go, Dad. Thanks for asking. Oh, wait. He hadn't asked me. His purpose was to pull Mom away from Seri because Mom fuelled Seri's panicked state. Mom would sit for hours while Seri calmed down after weird times like this, never leaving her side. It had been seventeen years, and this technique wasn't working. Time for Dad and his no tolerance for shit regime. The kid gloves had to come off with Seri. The drama was too much for us.

Seri wiped her eyes, blew her nose for the hundredth time that day (another habit that drove us nuts, but at least now it was justified) and followed Dad out the door.

It was then Mom noticed my existence.

"I'm really proud of you, Ivy. That hug meant a lot to your sister. I saw it in her face."

I should have known the conversation would still be about Seri. "Well, anything we can do for Seri." Sarcasm oozed out with every word.

"What do you mean by that? I was trying to give you a compliment. What did I do wrong this time to annoy you?"

Mom looked tired, old at this moment. Deep black circles darkened the skin beneath her eyes, and they didn't hold the same warmth they once did. I didn't think it was fair to heap more on her by being a whiny nincompoop.

"Nothing, Mom. I love you." I hugged her and held her for a moment. I always felt like the adult in this situation because I towered over her, and she rested her head on my shoulder. I held her like I had needed to be held earlier.

"There, there, little one," I teased as I patted her head.

Mom laughed heartily and took a playful swat at me. "You aren't too big for a smack, little lady. You'll always be my baby no matter how tall you are! I have to run to the flower shop. Want to come?"

A part of me did, but the other part was scared she might talk about Seri again. I was not in the mood to hear about her any more tonight. I wanted to grieve a bit for my hopes that had been dashed less than an hour ago. I wanted someone to hug me and tell me things would be okay but didn't want to beg for attention.

"I don't think so, Mom. I'm going to head to my room and read. I'm in the middle of a great book."

"Ok, Ives. I'll be in to say good night to you later. I promise."

I didn't plan on holding my breath, and I wasn't surprised when I heard Mom close Seri's door later in the evening after saying good night to her. When I heard Mom's bedroom door close for the final time, I wondered if she was aware of the broken promise she had tucked me in with for the night.

Seri

Supper had been nice. It was rare lately to sit down as a family at the supper table to enjoy a meal. Dad had been working a lot lately, and Mom was busy in the garden as this was harvesting time, so Ivy and I usually sat in the living room, scarfing down our food and watching the latest Netflix fad.

We talked about nothing and everything during supper. I had been feeling good until Ivy asked Mom if she had gotten an email yet. It was like a light switch flipped in my head. Instead of dark to light, my mind went from quiet to noisy in an instant. Doubt and fear inched its way up my spine.

Trying to shake off those feelings, I got up and started to wash the dishes. Ivy and I usually fought over who was going to wash but tonight, I needed the distraction. I needed something to focus on, and fighting with Ivy about whose turn it was would only rile me up more.

I grabbed the dirtiest dish I could find and began scrubbing when I heard Dad.

"Hey, Ives, you are AAA in our book."

Oh, no. Poor Ivy. I had seen how hard she had worked. After the first cut, Ivy was still with me in the tryout process. She picked up momentum with each passing session. She had been the one to ask me to do shooting with her in the yard. She even went running with me. I had asked her again the other night to do sprints, but she told me not to get carried away. That her body had to adjust to the effort she had been putting in. Only Ivy. She had the ability to make me laugh like no one else but right now, I didn't feel like laughing. I felt like crying. Ivy would take this hard, and that hurt my heart. I wanted to console her, but The Voice had other ideas.

"Well, I guess you're going to have to quit, Seri. You might have made it, but we both know you can't sustain it."

I wasn't the least bit surprised to hear The Voice. My gut churned. The hamster was about to hop on its wheel and start its relentless spinning. That's what I sometimes pictured in my head when The Voice spoke to me. I saw a fat, brown, furry hamster running in its wheel trying with all its might to make progress but getting nowhere. That's how I felt with my thoughts. They circled around and around in my mind, but I couldn't get away from them.

I put all my effort into scrubbing the frying pan. Go away. Go away. I repeated this in my head to drown out the negativity, but it was to no avail. The Voice was persistent. It overtook me.

"You can't do it, Seri; not without Ivy. You can't. Tell them. Tell them before it's too late, and they make you go back."

I wasn't sure how long I stood there struggling before I felt Mom rubbing my back. I had no idea what I said out loud or if it was taking place in my mind. All I knew was I couldn't play without Ivy. It just wasn't possible. I needed her. She was my rock.

She anchored me more than she realized. I couldn't play in a new rink with a new coach and new teammates. I wasn't cut out for AAA.

"I can't. I can't. I can't." I tried to say something else, but nothing came out. I remembered when I was younger and had felt overwhelmed, Mom rocked me back and forth. It subdued my thoughts and gave me comfort. I slowly rocked back and forth, waiting for comfort. None came.

Ivy approached like in a dream. Poke. Did she just poke me in the nose? What was she saying? I couldn't hear her over my thoughts. I felt Mom rubbing my back, and her stress transferred to me with every stroke. Her nervous energy fuelled my unease, yet I needed her to stand by me, or I would have crumbled to the floor.

It wasn't until I felt Dad's hands guiding me to a chair at the kitchen table that I was able to speak. I wanted to apologize to Ivy. I wanted to tell her how proud of her I was. That she had worked hard, and she was an amazing player. But my mind stifled all those thoughts, and what came out instead, were my fears.

"I can't. I can't go back without Ivy." I gulped at the air like a drowning rat. "I won't have anyone with me. Not Dad. Not Ivy. I will let you all down. I'm not good enough to play AAA." There. I had told them exactly what my mind was telling me. What they needed to know. That I was not the player they thought I was. I crumbled and found solace in Mom's lap.

I don't know how long a person can cry, but I didn't feel like I was able to stop. I felt the weight of the world on my shoulders yet again. I knew Dad wasn't going to understand. He would feel like I was wasting a good opportunity and tell me there was no quit in us. Mom would tell me I could do whatever made me happy but in her eyes, I would see the cost this took on her heart. She was the only person who fully saw my struggles, but she didn't understand what I struggled with. I couldn't tell her. It was too crazy. And Ivy, oh, Ivy. She had every right to hate me. She was cast to the side because of me. Another fresh batch of sobs wracked my body.

"This wouldn't be happening if you had stayed home in the first place, Seri. You need to stop fighting me." The self-righteous voice enjoyed my pain.

"Seri? I love you, Seri." It was Ivy's voice pulling me back to reality. Away from The Voice.

"I will be there as your number one fan. I'll come to every game and cheer like Mom does." I laughed in spite of myself. It was more of a snort, but it pulled me from the lure of The Voice for a moment. I pictured Ivy acting like our mother at the rink. Ivy was way funnier, and I imagined what would come out of her.

Mom piped up and told Ivy she resembled that remark, which widened my smile. I swiped at my running nose and grabbed a Kleenex. Dad was taking me to the store, and it was a much-needed distraction from what had just taken place. I blew my nose not just because it was running, but because it was a giant germ catcher and needed to be emptied often, then headed out the door with Dad. He asked if I wanted to drive, but I didn't feel emotionally stable to get behind the wheel, so I declined.

The drive to the store was done in silence. I hadn't expected that. I thought for sure he would have asked what was wrong and that maybe for the first time, I could open up and tell him.

We picked up milk and as usual when I went to the store with Dad, he wanted junk food that none of us needed. Mom teased him that he was a junk food junkie and couldn't be trusted to bring home anything healthy. She always sent him to the store on a budget, but he found a way around that. If we needed milk, he would buy two litres instead of four and use the rest of the cash for a chocolate bar.

Tonight was no exception. He got milk for his cereal, but the chips and starburst candy were his idea.

The sun was setting, and the night air was crisp and refreshing. The parking lot was almost empty. We strolled silently across the lot to our car. I found it hard to believe on such a beautiful and peaceful evening, I had melted down less than an hour ago. The night air and sun setting relaxed me.

Dad started the car but instead of putting it in gear and taking off, he turned to me. I couldn't read him and was unsure of what he was going to say.

"Seri. I don't know you anymore, kid. I never know what you are thinking, or what you may do next. Help me understand what's eating at you. We need to deal with whatever it is because it's tearing our family apart."

The point-blank declaration made me speechless. The last sentence stuck in my mind like popcorn between teeth. I was tearing the family apart? It felt like that lately, and he confirmed it. My worry and doubts weren't wrong. He was verifying my worst fears.

"I – I don't know, Dad. I'm sorry I'm a burden," was all I could say.

"You're not a burden. Don't you understand that? But I don't know who you are anymore. I see my little girl trapped inside a cloud of misery, and I don't get why. Help me with that, Seri. Please. Help me understand what you are thinking." Sadness filled his voice. I had never heard it before. I debated telling him about The Voice.

"Don't, Seri. He won't get it," came the reply.

"I... It's too hard to explain, Dad. You won't understand. I don't understand."

Frustration overtook him. "Jesus, Seri. That's always your answer, and it's selfish! Pure selfish! Every single day, I watch you wilt into this feeble girl with no self-esteem and no desire to leave the house to do anything! Your mother doesn't know how to do anything unless it involves you, and you can't see past your own nose!" A flood gate opened, and he was unable to hold back. "Damn it, Seri! It should have been us comforting Ivy tonight. She needed her mom to wrap her arms around her and tell her she was proud of her but instead, we had to deal with your issues, and we don't have a fucking clue what those issues are!"

Dad rammed the car into gear and jerked out of the parking lot and onto the road. I had never seen him so frustrated.

"Say something, Seri. Please, tell me. What is your problem?"

"I – I don't know how to tell you. I..." I struggled to find words to identify the presence I had become so familiar with. "I have this voice... It's in my head. It's been there for a long time." I turned slowly and looked at his face. I needed to see his reaction. "It – it tells me things. It tells me I'm not worthy." I couldn't believe I had finally said that out loud. The Voice was silenced momentarily, most likely shocked I had finally shared my dirty secret with someone. All of a sudden, weight came off my chest. Hope seeped in for the first time in...

"Are you kidding me, Seri? A voice? What the hell are you talking about?"

As fast as the hope had come, it disappeared. The disbelief in his voice silenced me. His reaction was what I had feared for years. That I would be ridiculed. That I would feel crazy. And I did. I felt nuts. I felt like I was losing control, and I was never going to get it back.

"I didn't say it right. I mean, my thoughts are negative, and I don't know how to change that." The Voice was back, laughing softly in the corner of my mind. It had been right. No one would believe it was real. It was laughing louder. My hand gripped the door handle and for an instant, I thought of opening the door and hopping out. I had come this far though and didn't want to give up. One last try.

"Dad, I think I'd like to talk to someone. Maybe a therapist who could help me decipher what I'm thinking."

"What good is a therapist if you can't even tell me? What can they help you with that I can't?"

I didn't know how to answer that. I didn't know how to tell him I wasn't who he thought I was, and I didn't want him to think less of me than he did right now. What I was feeling was not a reflection on his parenting, but I had a feeling that was what he was thinking. I didn't want him to feel inadequate. I knew that feeling all too well. "Nothing I guess. I thought they could tell me what seems to be going on with me."

"Well, whatever it is, whatever is going on, you need to stop it. Do you hear me, Seri? It's time to get tough with you. I've tried to reason with you. Your mother bends over backwards for you, but it's time we handle this like grown ups. If you are having negative thoughts, change them! We all have negative thoughts sometimes, but we deal with them. You're seventeen years old, and you need to act like it. From now on, we put this shit behind us and get back to who we used to be, okay?"

I nodded and hoped he saw me. I didn't trust myself not to break down if I spoke. I was scared of what his reaction would be if I did. He had never spoken to me like this before. Ever. I had always been his pride and joy. We had always enjoyed an easy, fun relationship, and I had ruined it.

Dad and I didn't speak again that night, but I talked to Mom when she came in to check on me. I told her I couldn't play AAA. She was not surprised by this. She simply nodded and told me I could step down to AA if I agreed to get a job this coming summer.

She always tried to negotiate with me to keep me moving forward.

"Take the deal," The Voice told me. "We will worry about work when the time comes."

I agreed instantly but couldn't shake the feeling I was getting a lousy deal out of this. I was stepping back from something I loved so much for something I didn't want to do. I didn't want to work. I wanted to play AAA hockey. However, The Voice was content with the bargain and when it was content, I had momentary peace. Peace of mind was something I longed for more than anything.

A few weeks later, I joined Dad's team, but he made little effort to talk to me, and I had no idea what to say to him. Ivy sensed something was off and did her best to bridge the gap between us. Very slowly, Dad and I started making small talk on the way to practices, and things started to return to normal between us. Neither of us mentioned me stepping away from AAA or the conversation that night in the car. It was too painful for either of us to deal with.

October 12th, 2017

Adalynn

It was my least favourite thing to do: close down my little shop for the winter, but it had to be done. It was early October, and my produce had been harvested and sold. I thought of selling different knick-knacks and gardening supplies throughout the winter but with the cost to keep things afloat, it wasn't feasible. Not only that, I feared I'd grow weary of the business venture. When the spring breeze blew its first mighty breath, it filled me with joy, and I sensed gardening time was near. It gave me a sense of purpose and ignited my passion. I didn't want to lose that or for it to grow old by being open year-round.

I tilled the grounds yesterday and was applying the last bit of straw over the freshly-planted garlic. I loved nothing better than seeing the garlic poke its head up in early spring. Another tell-tale sign I waited for with anticipation.

I glanced at my watch to see the time and was not surprised to learn three hours had flown by. It was four o'clock. Time was irrelevant when I was in the garden. I had a habit of losing hours every time I stepped foot in it, and I loved it that way. Soon though, the girls and Dex would be home from hockey, and they would be hungry. Bittersweet emotions followed that thought. It was great they were on the same team again this year but heartbreaking at the same time that Seri had decided to step back from AAA after Ivy had been cut.

The night Ivy had been cut, I knew Seri wouldn't play AAA. Whatever she battled with daily was not going to allow her to continue without knowing anyone on the team. No other girl from our area had cracked the roster and without Ivy and Dex on the bench, it was not going to happen for Seri. I had seen that look of panic too many times and seen her lose too many inner battles to think this time was going to be different. I don't know what had transpired between Dex and Seri the night they went to the store, but it hadn't been good. Neither of them had spoken to each other for weeks afterwards and although they were talking now, there was distance between them. I wasn't sure how to help. Frankly, I wasn't a help to anyone anymore. The thought depressed me, but I stifled it because my garden was no place for bad thoughts.

I took one last look around the garden, soaked in its beauty, turned and headed towards the house. I was surprised to find Dex standing on the patio watching me. I smiled and asked him where the girls were.

"They decided to hang out at Andrea's for a bit after practice. Seri told me to tell you they would be home by five for supper."

"That's good for Seri. She needs to hang out with the girls. She's been going through a lot lately."

He was annoyed that I said that but held his tongue. I changed the subject. No good ever came from us discussing our daughter. I washed my hands at the outdoor sink, dried them and approached the patio.

"How's the team looking? Your first big game is next week." I didn't think, just walked over to him and stood on my tippy toes to kiss him on the cheek. An old habit I had forgotten until now. A familiar tingling coursed through me as I placed the kiss gently on his face. We didn't have many moments alone anymore. It felt nice. Our eyes met and held for a moment. Desire stirred in me. Crazy how being physically close to him had me feeling this kind of lust. He must have felt it too because he grabbed my hand to pull me back and kissed me softly on the lips. His hands shifted to the sides of my face and as the kiss deepened, all thoughts of the girls left me. All I could think of was how good it felt to be in his embrace.

My arms encircled him, pulling him closer. He was aroused already, and that fuelled my passion. I pushed him back a few steps, down onto our patio couch. Our lips parted long enough for him to sit and for me to straddle him. He pulled me down, one hand entangled in my hair, the other on my back. I devoured him. I took in his scent, kissed his lips, ran my fingers through his sexy beard.

It never got old how much I wanted him. How good his hands felt on every inch of my skin. His lips on my neck had my skin burning. I lifted my arms so he could pull off my shirt. Like magic, he slipped off my bra at the same time. I gasped as his tongue teased my nipples. His touch was intoxicating. I wanted more.

When I could handle it no longer, I quickly stood, discarded the rest of my clothes while he did the same. I was done with foreplay. I wanted him inside me. I felt like a teenager again, fumbling out of my clothes and smiling at him as I finished undressing.

Sitting in front of me naked in all his manhood was almost enough to send me over the edge. My smile vanished as I once again straddled the man I loved, and together we got lost in the ecstasy of the moment.

"That was a nice welcome home," he muttered when we were able to talk again.

I laughed as I pulled my leggings on. "It certainly was. Maybe you should leave and come back again," I playfully replied. This easy, carefree banter was a pleasant change. I loved these moments with Dex and lately, they were few and far between.

"I don't have the strength to leave again. I'm an old man now, Addie."

"You weren't too old a minute ago."

He laughed and tugged on my hair. "That's enough out of you. You're supposed to be a lady."

We made our way into the house and my mind returned to Seri. I wondered what she was doing, and if she was okay. I had no intentions of ruining the moment with Dex, so I kept my worries to myself. I wished Seri would talk to me and tell me what the hell she dealt with, but she refused to share. If she told me, I could help, and my worries would fade away. Not knowing what she dealt with left me feeling hopeless, and it was consuming my thoughts.

"Earth to Addie. Did you hear me?" Dex stood in front of the refrigerator, trying to get my attention.

"No, I didn't. Sorry. I was thinking of what your bare ass looked like," I joked and softly swatted his behind. "What did you say?"

I don't think he bought what I was selling, but he didn't press the issue.

"I asked if you wanted to go out for supper. Just you and me. We can shower and change, then enjoy a romantic evening. Maybe head to the boardwalk afterwards?" He was excited at the prospect of a date.

"What about the girls? Seri said she would be home at five, and we both know she won't be a minute late. You know how she gets if plans change." Instantly, I regretted what I had said. It took the wind out of his sails.

"Yeah, whatever. It was just an idea." He closed the fridge door and headed to our room. "We'll go another time."

Torn between chasing him down the hall and worrying about messing with Seri's routine, especially how sad she seemed lately, I stood frozen in my spot. Hopefully, Dex would understand why I worried so much after his initial hurt wore off. I wasn't convinced Seri would sleep well tonight if her routine changed. Routine was the only thing that gave her peace. I would make it up to Dexter another night when Seri was feeling more herself. I took the hamburg I had taken out of the freezer earlier and began making supper.

March 3rd, 2018

Dexter

I stood on the bench in the coldest rink in the land, watching my team warm up. We were in the final minutes of our warm-up before the league championship game started, and I think I was more nervous than the girls. We had finished second in the league behind our rivals the Wildlings. It was a rivalry that had grown over the last eight years and this year, I was determined to help the girls win the title. Each team had four championships to their name, so this year's title would give one team the right to call themselves the true champions. I'd be damned if it was going to be the Wildlings.

Hockey season had gone well. Ivy, Seri and I really enjoyed the season together. Ivy referred to us as the three amigos, and I think that was an accurate description. Addie didn't come to our practices, but she didn't miss a single game. I had to hand it to her; this year, she had been well behaved. Only one outburst had come from her but in her defence, a father from the opposing team had lost his mind, screaming at one of our players. He proceeded to call me an asshole, and she took great offence to that. She wasn't long telling him what she thought of him for yelling at children, and that if he was so perfect, why wasn't he a volunteer?

She had used her outdoor voice and a colourful vocabulary with wild hand gestures. I had seen the brouhaha from the bench and tried to pretend I didn't know her. Once I found out what had taken place, I was secretly proud of her but told her she should tone it down a bit next time. She apologized for her part in the

49

mess but stated the only person allowed to call me an asshole was her.

This season was special because this was the last year Ivy and Seri were eligible to play together. Seri would be too old next year to play minor hockey. As disappointed as I was she hadn't finished out her final year in AAA, another part of me was grateful for this last year together. I wouldn't tell Seri that because I didn't want her to think the decision she had made was one I agreed with. I still felt like she had thrown away her God-given talent for nothing. When Addie had come to bed the night Seri and I had our fight and told me she wasn't going back to AAA, I had been angry. My words had gone in one ear and out the other.

I looked around the ice and was impressed with what I saw. All eighteen girls had given me everything they had this year. They were as invested in winning as I was. Addie had told me once that the reason I was such an amazing coach (her words, not mine) was because I was more concerned with making every player better than I was concerned with winning. She was right. I loved watching a player develop their skills to the next level. But I loved to win too. It was beyond satisfying for me when both occurred in the same season.

The warm-up was over. We headed to the dressing room so the Zamboni could clean the ice in preparation for game time. I stood outside the dressing room door, fist bumping each girl as she walked by.

"Great job, Snoozer. Atta girl, Snipes. Nice shooting, Tex." I had a nickname for every player I had ever coached. This team was no exception. I called Ivy, Tex because of her wicked shot.

She could let that puck fly! I wasn't convinced I could handle her shot as a goalie, let alone being a girl her age in nets, with a puck coming at me at that kind of speed.

The last girl off the ice was always Seri and today was no exception.

"Awesome effort today, Chucky," I said.

Seri skated up for her high five and smiled at the nickname. Usually I used a kid's last name or a strong suit of theirs to make up their nickname, but Seri's had come from a tournament a few years back. She had been telling me before the game how nervous she was, and she thought maybe she was going to throw up. I told her to go out her first shift and go as hard as she could to get rid of the nervous energy, and she would feel fine after that. Well, she listened, but it did not do the trick. Instead, as she skated to the bench, she power puked through her helmet onto the ice and some of the players. It was not a highlight reel moment. I wasn't in her good books for a while after that, or Adalynn's either. I had to hand it to Seri; she didn't miss much time that game. She had gone to the dressing room, and Addie helped clean her up as best she could. Addie had asked Seri if she wanted to sit out the rest of the game, but she said, "I have to finish. I can't let the team or Dad down."

When Seri came back to the bench, I was pleasantly surprised and wary. None of us wanted a repeat of what had just happened. I asked her, "You sure you can play, Chucky?" The whole team laughed, Seri included. The name stuck.

I shifted my focus to giving Seri a high five.

"Thanks, coach," Seri replied and headed into the dressing room.

Time for my pregame talk.

As per usual, Seri sat in the corner of the room where only one person could sit beside her, and that person was always either Ivy or Mari. Today it was Mari. Mari was Seri's best friend. She was a nice kid with a big heart. She liked everyone, and she was never put out by Seri's quiet attitude or sharp tongue. Maybe that was why they fit so well together. They complimented each other like salt and pepper. Peanut butter and jam. Mari certainly brought the best out of Seri and any kid that could make Seri smile, was a great person in my eyes.

Ivy was in the centre of the room, in the middle of the action. No shocker there. She was loud and proud. Sometimes too loud, and it drove me crazy she called me Coach Dad instead of just coach. She told me it felt like she was demoting me if she didn't add dad after saying coach. I had given up that argument a long time ago. She looked ready to play, and that was a good thing because she could fire up the girls when she wanted to.

My talk was short and sweet. Play like they could and they would win. Play with heart. Heart and hard work trumps talent every day, all day. Lucky for them, they had all three. Heart, work ethic and talent. I fired up the girls and as my voice kept rising, my adrenaline did too.

I glanced around the room, and the girls were ready, even Seri. She was talking to Mari, and they gave each other a fist bump and headed to the centre of the room. Time for the team cheer.

"ONE. TWO. THREE. THRASHERS!!"

Just like that, the game began. Lots of games are described as nail-biters, but this one had me on the edge of the bench the entire time. Our nerves got the best of us and before the clock ticked off three minutes, we were losing 2-0. I had only one time out and was not happy I had to use it so soon, but I had to settle the girls down before we dug ourselves a hole we couldn't get out of.

"Girls, now that you got that out of your system, let's settle in and play our game. Let's help Molly. She made a few great saves already. Let's build on the foundation of those saves and switch the momentum."

The time-out paid off. We dominated the remaining first period with all the action in our offensive zone. We outshot them 22 to 11, but we couldn't solve the riddle, and that riddle was their goalie. She was terrific. She was fast across the crease and came out of her net to cut off the angles we normally scored from.

In between period one and two, I spoke again. "We are only going to score on her today with passing and garbage goals. We have to get to the front of the net and dig. Get the two on ones working for us. Fake your shot, move the puck. That's how we're gonna start filling the net."

As usual, the girls listened to what I said and applied it on the ice. Kia opened up the scoring with a beautiful cross-ice pass from Seri halfway through the second period. It breathed life into the girls, and they stepped up their game. So much so, we got our second and game tying goal just as the buzzer signalled to end the period. Seri was the one to fill the net this time, going end to end. A proud father and coach moment.

The last period was filled with the most action. The Wildlings scored again making it 3-2, but we answered with a goal of our own. Seri was on fire, got the puck back to Mari who fired it low, and Jesse tipped in the shot. With five minutes left, we finally took the lead with Seri firing a wrist shot top corner. I had never seen her so determined.

She wasn't alone in her grit. Every girl was doing their part and playing the game of their lives. There wasn't a person on our team or parent in the stand that wanted to lose to the Wildlings. I didn't mind losing to any other team in our league, but not to these guys. They were not graceful winners.

When the clock ticked down and displayed ten seconds left, I thought the game was ours. They had a player advantage because they pulled their goalie, but I saw how determined the girls were to win.

We iced the puck to take off the pressure, and the play got whistled down. The linesman got ready to drop the puck for what I guessed would be the final time. The puck hit the ice, bounced towards the Wildling's centre, and she poked it through her legs to the D who was waiting and ready to fire a slap shot. The Wildling defence player couldn't shoot like Ivy, but she had a shot that was nothing to laugh at.

I saw the puck in slow motion. The Wildling wound up and let go. Her stick bent as it connected with the ice and the puck. The puck shot past Ivy, who dove to try to block it, and past Molly's left shoulder, hitting the net top shelf. I couldn't believe my eyes. They had tied the game with four seconds left. Four measly seconds. I didn't want the girls to dwell on this untimely misfortune. I clapped each one on the back and told them the game was a long piece from over.

Four seconds was long enough to drop the puck at centre ice and watch the clock run out. No player made any effort to move, knowing overtime was going to decide the winner of this game.

I hated overtime, but I hated shoot outs even more. I was happy we were playing a four on four format but wasn't looking forward to how the rest of overtime would play out. Four on four would be played for five minutes. If no team scored, then it went to three on three for five minutes, then two on two, and then one on one until a winner was determined. That was a lot of pressure to put on a young athlete as it was a team sport. One on one was an unfair way to decide a hockey game in my opinion, but I was confident these girls were going to handle their business in the first OT.

I was wrong. No winner was decided in the first fifteen minutes of overtime, so unfortunately the game was going to be decided with the one on one format. I had to decide who to start. Which girl I thought could take us all the way. I had several excellent choices, but I decided to go with Seri. Not only because she had been focused all game, but because I thought this could be the moment she needed to triumph over whatever self doubt picked away at her.

"Seri, can you go?" I asked instead of demanding, hoping to put her at ease in this tough situation. Her teammates agreed with this choice and started cheering her on but for the first time this game, Seri hesitated.

"I don't know, coach. Maybe start with someone else."

Not the answer I had expected. I had to pull her off the ice most of the game, and now she was hesitating when we needed her most. I understood nerves. Hell, I had them right now as the coach, but what I didn't get was letting those nerves dictate how we ran our life. I pulled her to the side.

"If you're nervous, Seri, that's good. It means you care. You're a big reason we came this far. All you can do is go out and do your best. I believe in you. Remember what I told you. It's time you believe in yourself. Buck up. You got this."

Her bottom lip trembled, and a tear escaped down her cheek. Damn it. I didn't know if it was a good idea to put her out. I shifted into the centre of our huddle as the whistle blew to signal the start of the fourth OT.

"Does anyone else want to go out? Start this overtime?" No one piped up.

Mari broke the silence. "I think it should be Seri. She deserves the chance to win for us after how she played today. Go get it, Seri!"

The bench erupted into cheers, and Seri reluctantly made her way to centre. I didn't have a good feeling about this. Not about the effort she was about to put in but the ramifications this might have if it didn't go in our favour. Too late, the puck dropped, and the final OT began.

Seri won the draw, picked up the puck, skated by her opponent and took a shot on net. The goalie made an unbelievable save, and the rebound went up over the net. Seri and the Wildling player rushed behind the net to get the puck but as Seri leaned in to get it, the Wildling's stick went between her legs and hooked her down.

The refs didn't see the hook as intentional and after playing it back in my mind a thousand times, it wasn't, but the outcome was the same. Seri fell to the ice. It was in that split second fall, the Wildling won the puck battle and took off like a shot. She was on a clear, uncontested breakaway. It was up to Molly. The Wildlings had been shooting low all game, using deflections in front to try and score their goals. I assumed that was going through Molly's mind when she went down into the butterfly before the puck left the girl's stick. I can't explain the sickening feeling when the puck went up and over Molly's trapper. My heart went to Molly and Seri. In no way had this been their fault. They had done everything they could. Seri had almost caught the shooter on the back check, which was nothing short of an extraordinary effort. As sick in my gut as I felt for all these girls, I was proud of every single one of them.

"Hold your head up, girls. Go give Molly and Seri some love." Most of the girls were crying. I had yet to look at Seri. I felt somehow responsible for this disastrous outcome. She hadn't wanted to go out, but I had pushed her. Would I have done that to any other player? Or had I done that because it was my daughter?

Seri hadn't gotten up off the ice. She was wracked in sobs. As much as this hurt now, we would see that second in the league was still an honour. But today it hurt. I went to Seri, helped her up and hugged her as hard as I ever had.

"You did good today, kid. I am proud to be your coach and your father." My words fell on deaf ears. She was inconsolable. I let go as the girls huddled around her and Molly. They each said how happy they were to be on this team, win, lose or draw, and that's when the hurt in my gut eased. We weren't able to say we were the number one team this year, but we sure as hell were champs. Their effort and, most of all, their supportive team attitudes was what mattered the most.

We stood on the blue line, accepted our silver medals and made our way to the dressing room. Before I went in, I went to find Adalynn. As much as she drove me crazy hovering over Seri, Seri needed her. I should have known Addie would be close by. She was standing a few feet away from the dressing room. She looked heartbroken.

"Hey, I want to talk to the girls for a minute, then I'll let parents in to see them. They could use the support. Can you come in and be there in case Seri needs you?"

Adalynn nodded yes but made no attempt to talk to me. Was she angry at me for putting Seri out? Now was not the time to ask. Besides, I knew the answer.

The scene was completely different from last year when we had won the championship. Gone was the laughter, squirting water bottles over each other and cheers, replaced with tears, hugs and hanging heads. Losing was a part of life, but I didn't like it one damn bit. I told the girls to remember that learning to lose was just as important as winning. It taught us how to be graceful in defeat. I wanted to kick over the garbage can, but that would have been hypocritical of me, so I stifled the urge.

As I looked around the room for the last time, a profound sadness washed over me. Not only for Seri, who looked devastated, but for every girl in the room. I watched these girls grow up in front of my very eyes. To me, they were like my own daughters. They had blossomed into wonderful young ladies and there was nothing more I could teach them. Those days were gone. I had coached most of them since they were five years old, and saying good-bye to them was harder than the loss we had just endured.

I stuck around for a few more minutes, made sure to say good-bye to every player, and then went outside to start the car. The girls would be warm until they got into the chilly air. Then they would complain they were cold, and I'd have to crank the heat. I thought I would get ahead of them today. Maybe help ease their hurt some with a warm vehicle.

It was ten minutes before Ivy appeared. That was new. Ivy was never the first, especially in our family. She threw her gear into the trunk and plunked down in the backseat.

"Tough loss today, Coach Dad. Real tough." The emotion in Ivy's voice hit hard, and I was struck by how far she had come as a player and a teammate.

"Sure was, Ives. But I meant what I said in there today. I loved every minute of coaching you guys. I was inspired by your dedication and how much you grew as a person and player this year."

"Geez, Dad, don't get gushy. I'm already trying not to blubber back here."

And just like that, the mood felt lighter.

"My bad. Second place is actually the first losers, and your gear stinks so bad my eyes are watering. There, is that better?" I teased.

Ivy laughed. "Well, that sounds more like you. Leave the mushiness to Mom."

Addie appeared at the mention of her name, but not with Seri. When she opened the car door, I asked where Seri had gotten to.

"She went to the bathroom. Said she'd be out in a minute." Adalynn looked distraught, doing all she could not to cry.

"I guess she isn't doing good?" I asked.

"You guessed right. As if she didn't already feel the weight of the world on her shoulders." She threw her arms in the air. "This had to happen."

I had no reply to that, and I couldn't tell if she was angry with me, the situation or Seri's inability to process things of this scope. For most athletes, today's game was hard to digest, but for Seri...? I could only imagine what she was thinking, and how she was processing this. She had absolutely nothing to be upset about, but no one would be able to tell her otherwise.

"Maybe getting MVP will make her feel better about the game," said Ivy. "They don't give those to the worst player. I'd have way more in my collection if that was the case." She was trying to ease Addie's worry. "Everyone on the team told Seri and Molly a hundred times not to feel like it was their fault. I could have ended the game in the third when I fired that slap shot that hit the goalie square in the lips. Three inches to the right, and we would've been celebrating, not crying." She paused, then added, "I bet that goalie hears bells ringing in her ears for the next week."

Her comment made Adalynn smile, and she turned to Ivy. "First of all, you are never the worst player, and secondly, I love you, Ivy. You know that, right? You did so good today."

Ivy smiled ear to ear. "Thanks, mamma bear. You did good in the stands too."

We waited another five minutes before Seri trotted out of the rink, all alone with her head down. She gently tossed her gear into the trunk and slid into the backseat as quietly as she could. She bit her bottom lip so hard, she almost drew blood.

"Hey, fellow glum chum," said Ivy. "Want to eat our blues away and convince Mom and Dad to eat somewhere?"

"No. I just want to go home." Seri clenched her hands together in a tight ball and squeezed her eyes shut. She rocked ever so slightly. With her lips moving with silent words, it seemed like she was chanting.

"We need to eat, Seri," I started to say, but Adalynn cut me off.

"Just go home, Dex. I'm not hungry either."

Well, that was that. There was no reaching Seri in the state she was in. What had started out as a terrific day was ending where most of our days were ending up lately. In the shitter.

Seraphina

I couldn't believe I had lost the face-off draw. I knew as soon as the puck went to their defenceman, she was going to score and tie the game. The Wildings were not a team to quit, and they sure weren't quitting today.

All game long, I had been focussed. The Voice couldn't break through my level of concentration, and I was able to think of nothing but playing the game I loved with an amazing group of friends. Especially Mari. We had met when we were in our first year of hockey and had been as thick as thieves ever since.

Mari understood me better than I understood myself. When I got bitchy from feeling uncomfortable, instead of being put off by that or insulted, she pushed back, easing me into uncomfortable situations. She knew when to give it back, and also when to give me space. Understanding my uncertainty, she made sure to include me in everything. It was like she knew I feared rejection. I never told Mari the depth of my struggles, but it was like she could see into my head.

The only person who could read me like Mari was my mom. Mom stifled me at times, whereas Mari gave me the right amount of space to help me figure out how to deal with things that made me uncomfortable.

I looked at Mari and saw the crestfallen look on her face as she realized the game was tied.

"The pressure is getting to you, Seri. You should have won the face-off."

The Voice didn't miss the opportunity to kick me while I was down. I skated to centre ice and as the puck dropped, my legs felt like lead. My energy had been sucked out of me. Overtime was always daunting, but this was going to be twice as hard if The Voice started its crap. Four on four was the format for the first overtime period. That didn't make me overly anxious but as the overtimes kept slipping away and we eliminated a player with each round, my heart raced faster than it should. Sweat oozed out of my pores, not from exertion but from the apprehensive feeling I couldn't shake.

"Well, it's one on one time. Let's hope your dad is smart enough not to call on you."

I wanted to scream. I wanted to tell myself to fuck off. I had just played one of the best games of my life. Why couldn't I see that? I didn't hear Dad talking to the team until he bent over and pulled me to the side.

"Seri, can you go?"

"This is a baaaaad idea, Seri. Your team wants this badly..." The Voice sounded concerned, like it cared if we won or lost.

"I don't know, coach," I heard myself reply. "Maybe start with someone else." I glanced up at Dad, who was baffled by my answer. He gave me words of encouragement and after he said, "All you can do is go out and do your best," the voice interrupted him.

"Your best, Seri? Your best won't be good enough. You just coughed up the puck, and now you think you can handle things out there alone. Come on. Take a seat so you don't ruin things. Tell your dad no."

Dad asked the team if anyone else wanted to start, and the only one who said anything was Mari. She thought I should start, and the rest of the team supported that decision.

"They must see something in me," I whispered to the voice.

"Ok, but don't say I didn't warn you." The Voice went silent.

The problem with The Voice was most times it was right. Today was no exception. When the stick went between my legs and I went down hard on the ice, I didn't need to hear The Voice to understand the validity of its premonition. I had failed. I had let down my dad, my other coaches and teammates. Because I couldn't stand up, I had lost the championship game. Scrambling to my feet, I tried to recover. I almost caught up to the Wildling player, but almost only counted in horseshoes and hand grenades. The sound of the goal reached my ears before I saw the puck go into the net, and I collapsed to the ice, defeated.

"Look what you made Molly go through, Seri. Are you happy now? When are you going to listen to me?"

I was crushed. The weight of the world pounced on me, and I wasn't strong enough to withstand it. I don't know how long I lay on the ice crying. I remembered Dad picking me up and trying to comfort me. It was me who should have been telling him how sorry I was. How I should have stayed on the bench.

I was in total shock when my name was called for MVP.

"Must have been daddy's pick." The snide remark came from my own thoughts. This time, I was not going to argue. Where did that get me? When had The Voice ever been wrong? I was beginning to see things as The Voice did, and that frightened me because I was not well liked by this beast that controlled me.

The events that followed were a blur. I remembered the girls hugging me and Molly, and telling us they loved us, and that we win and lose as a team. I wanted desperately to take solace in their words, but I couldn't shake the horrid picture that had been painted in my mind. I wanted to comfort Molly but couldn't find the words. She hadn't let us down. She was the best goalie in the league, and everyone knew it. Leaving the rink, she seemed upbeat, so I left well enough alone. I don't know what I would have done if she had told me it was my fault. I deserved it, but I couldn't handle any more today.

Mom was outside the dressing room and for the first time I could remember, I didn't want her around. I never thought of her as a liar but clearly after today, she needed to stop feeding me bullshit. I wasn't a great player. I wasn't a good kid or a normal teenager with typical problems. None of what I felt was normal! The Voice in my head was not typical! I was drowning, and she was pushing my head under the water further.

Before she spoke, I said, "I'm going to the bathroom. You can go to the car."

I didn't wait to hear her reply. I pushed past her and headed to the washroom. Thank my lucky stars, the bathroom was private, no stalls, just one toilet in a room by itself. I shut the door and broke down again.

"God, if you can hear me, I need you." I said a silent prayer. "I can't do this anymore. I can't keep living if all I do is ruin everything. I am lost. Please, please help me." I had never prayed before. Mom did, and we went to church with her up until a few years ago, but I had never felt important enough to God for him to hear me. I needed him to listen now.

Unsure if God had heard my pleas, I picked myself up off the floor. I splashed water on my face, wiped it dry with a hard brown piece of paper towel and headed to the car. I was grateful Mom had listened to me. She meant well, but I couldn't handle anyone right now.

I kept my head down and walked straight to the car. Someone called my name, but I didn't want to talk to anyone. It was rude to ignore whomever it was, but I wanted to get home to my bed and hide from the world. It must have been a satisfying idea because The Voice stayed silent.

The second I sat in the car, Ivy started talking. "Hey, fellow glum chum. Want to eat our blues away and convince Mom and Dad to eat somewhere?"

"Tell her to be quiet." The Voice was back. "Tell her you are going straight home." I obediently did as I was told.

"I just want to go home."

Are you satisfied? I snapped at The Voice. Ivy was doing her best to console me, and I was being a complete jerk. I simply couldn't stop it. I wanted to curl up in a ball and hide from the world but since I was still in the car, I settled for closing my eyes and silently repeating, "Please leave me alone," over and over.

No one spoke the rest of the way home. Not even The Voice.

Ivy

It was a very long, quiet drive home. Driving home from anywhere always seemed to take longer than getting to a destination but today, it felt like we had been driving for a full day, and we had just pulled onto the highway with 97 kms looming ahead. At least that was according to Betsy, my clever name for our GPS lady.

Losing was never fun, but today's game had meant a lot to our team. Minor hockey was coming to an end for over half of the girls. They would be aging out, either heading to university hockey or quitting altogether. We wanted badly to end our nine years together with a victory. For our family, it was the last championship game Seri would ever play in. The last time she and I would play hockey together until beer league when we got older. Not that beer league wasn't going to be fun. It was just that with minor hockey coming to an end, so was our family time at the rink. Mom and Dad weren't going to be present at the beer league like they were now, and that made me sad (Mom might come and cheer us on. She still tried to sit by me at the dentist). It was the one thing our family had done together since we were little, and knowing it was over was tough enough today. Factor in the loss, and it was a real bummer.

I knew better than to start a conversation with anyone on the way home. That was rough for someone like me who liked to converse. Mom looked on the verge of tears, Dad was staring at the road as if it was his first time driving and his concentration was imperative to our survival, and Seri was lost in her own world. It was ironic that I could reach out and touch her, but she was as far away from me as the moon.

With the age difference being less than a year between us, Seri and I had grown up doing everything together. There was no one in this world who understood me better than she did. She could read me like a second grade novel. She knew when I was sad, mad, annoyed or happy. From my facial expression, she could tell how I did on a test before I told her. She understood my love for sports was different than it was for most kids who played, but she loved having me on her team despite that. I loved being funny, but sometimes it was a defence mechanism for my insecurity, and she understood that. She thought I was hilarious (who didn't) but this last year, I didn't know how to make her smile. I couldn't figure out how to talk to her.

I liked to think I knew Seri but the more I thought of her on this incredibly long and freakishly-silent journey home, I realized I didn't know as much about her as she did me. That made me feel both sad and guilty. But how could I get to know somebody who didn't tell me what they were really thinking. She struggled at times but with what, I had no clue. It was obvious she didn't want to let any of us in on it, but I couldn't figure out why. That was what family was for. I was blessed with the gift of gab (I came by it honestly from my mother), and I suddenly realized I had done most of the talking when I was with my sister. The times I hadn't felt like talking, there hadn't been many conversations about her likes or dislikes or passions. She kept those things pretty quiet. She seemed afraid to share her thoughts.

I sometimes felt like she wasn't in control of what she was thinking. That sounded dumb even to me, but it was how I felt. Like she wanted to believe she was a great person, but that was not how she acted. It was like something was telling her otherwise. What I knew for absolute certain was her favourite thing was staying home and hanging out with family. I saw it in her demeanour. Nothing relaxed her more than being at home. It was her happy place. It was where I saw her laugh her grand-belly laugh with no inhibitions. Where I felt her kindness and saw her true-self. I loved being home too, but not like Seri did. It was where her mind seemed to rest. There was an edge to her when we were at other places, even the rink. Like she was nervous something was going to go wrong.

And boy did things go wrong today. Wowsers. I couldn't have drawn up a worse scenario to go wrong for Seri if I tried. This was worse than how she got her nickname Chucky. Incredibly, it was even worse than the time I had farted doing sit-ups at the AAA hockey tryouts in front of a girl I had just met. She had been holding my feet down. I prayed she hadn't heard the escape of my not-so quiet ass air as I struggled to sit up. When she said, "It's okay; keep going," I wanted to fall into the floor and disappear. I closed my eyes, praying that if I couldn't see her, she couldn't see me, and I kept going like she had asked. Not wanting to traumatize her further, I clenched my buns extra tight and luckily, I kept going without incident.

I had bounced back from that debacle, but I didn't know how Seri was going to keep going from this loss. In comparison, I felt my situation had been more dire than losing the way we had, but Seri wasn't going to understand that or realize we lost as a team. She wasn't going to factor in that no one was able to score in the overtime periods, and that the Wildling goalie had played the game of her friggin' life. She had robbed Seri on the shot in the final OT. That started the domino effect. That shot should have hit top corner, but the goalie had stuck her face in the puck's path. Seri wouldn't take into account the fact she was the biggest reason we had even gotten to overtime. She had either scored or assisted on every goal. The positive contributions she had made to the game wouldn't be considered. She would only factor in the failure, thinking she had let her entire team down, and she didn't process failure well. In fact, she didn't process feelings well in general. When she had been down on the ice crying, I had been unable to approach her. I had been afraid to fall apart in front of her and have her misinterpret my tears for disappointment in her. I was afraid she would think I was pitying her, and I didn't want to be blamed or responsible for making her feel worse. That happened sometimes.

Then there was my mother. Mom would somehow twist things I said to make it sound like it was my fault for revving Seri up or not taking her problems seriously enough. I can count on one hand, no, on my nose, how many times Mom had taken my side in a fight with Seri. So it had really surprised me Mom hadn't given me the "be nice to Seri; she's going through something" speech when she had gotten into the car. Mom hadn't even waited for Seri to come out of the rink, which was another rare phenomenon. Perplexing, really, considering this would be the one day I would have understood her reasons for waiting for Seri. Instead, Mom had remained silent with no words of comfort for any of us. With no words at all.

I took a sideways glance at Seri, saw her rocking ever so slightly, her eyes closed as tightly as I had clenched my butt on the fateful Assgate day, and I racked my brain for something, anything to say. Nothing came to me. Nothing seemed appropriate. I settled with reaching over and taking her hand. She surprised me by squeezing my hand so hard, I thought it might snap. When the only tear she shed on the way home slid slowly down her cheek, I was hopeful that maybe she didn't feel so alone and lost. I hoped she felt the support I was trying to channel through my hand, and I prayed she knew how much I loved her.

Adalynn

I didn't say one word the entire drive home. I had no idea what to say. So many emotions ran through me, I was afraid if I spoke I'd have a serious meltdown, and I didn't want to heap that baggage onto my girls. I was torn between being angry at Dexter for putting Seri into a position that had the power to affect her so deeply, fear that this would send her over the edge she had been teetering on for years and sadness that our years in hockey had to end on this note. It wasn't the loss that made it sad. It was the way in which it occurred.

When I had seen Seri skating to centre ice to start the one on one overtime, I shot out of the stands and ran along the boards in hopes of catching Dex's attention. To most, I looked like a meddling parent, but I didn't care. I only cared about Seri. I did not want her to take the ice. It wasn't that I didn't have faith she could win for us because I knew she could. Any of those girls could. They all had the talent to score.

The reason for the sudden spike in my blood pressure was that if she didn't score and the Wildlings did, she would not fair well mentally. I had seen the shift in her body when Dex had pulled her aside to talk to her before sending her out to slaughter. Could he not tell from his own daughter's body language that she didn't want to start the period? Damn it. I saw the change in her clear across the rink. Was he blind or in denial? Dex wanted her to succeed, but the risk was far greater than the reward in my eyes and when Seri went down on the ice, my heart dropped to the floor.

I didn't have to look in the backseat to know Seri was suffering. She had asked me to leave her alone in the rink, and that hurt me. I had always been there to cushion the blows for her, and now she was mad at me. Maybe she had every right to be mad. I was failing miserably as her mom.

My mind drifted to the local pool, where I became a bystander several years ago when a mother rushed into the water to save her drowning child. A poor swimmer, she struggled to keep afloat, so she handed her child an inflatable, but as soon as the child grabbed it, the air leaked out. I watched the child cling to the woman and drag her under. If not for the lifeguard, they both would have drowned. I felt the suffocation envelop me, and I understood how that mother felt. This was how I felt every day for the past year. Like an airless inflatable, a boulder on Seri's already overweighted shoulders, watching as she continued to drown with no trained lifeguard to rescue either of us. I had good intentions to help Seri, just no knowledge of how. Wasn't the path to hell paved with good intentions?

Every moment Seri suffered these past 12 years sped through my memory with each passing mile. Her first day of school, her incessant need to please us, her desire to constantly please everyone, her extreme disappointment with marks lower than 85, the look of sheer panic when trying something new, the way she made herself invisible in a crowd, her never being satisfied with who she was and only ever being truly happy at home. Memory after memory kept slamming into my mind, and it was all I could do not to scream. I shifted in my seat and tried to get a grip on my rising distress.

Staring out the car window, I thought back to the day in the doctor's office when I was asked if I was open to letting Seri see a mental health professional. I realized, six years ago, we had made a crucial error as parents. I should have said yes. Instead, we had brushed off the inclination that our daughter was struggling and forced her to carry a burden that no one should have had to carry alone. We associated her mental health with our shortcomings and wouldn't allow ourselves or Seri the chance to see what therapy could bring our family. We were too embarrassed to admit we couldn't help our child. But in our denial, we had failed our little girl. It was completely apparent that we were not equipped to deal with her issues on our own. I still had no idea what those issues were. We had let our stigma of mental health cloud our judgement, and we were paying serious consequences.

What felt like days later, we finally pulled into our driveway. Hopping out of the car, I headed to my shop instead of the house. I needed air. Before I talked to Seri, I needed space and time to think about what to say. I headed around back and walked to the shop.

I unlocked the door and marched straight to the storage room. It wasn't overly spacious. Each wall was lined with shelves, right up to the ceiling, giving me lots of room to store inventory. Yesterday, I had started unpacking the pots and plant food left over from last year. I decided now was a good time to bring the boxes out front and load up the store shelves.

I was in desperate need of a happy distraction. I was on the second box when I heard a noise behind me.

"What are you doing, Addie?" It was Dexter. He didn't have his usual swagger as he entered the shop. He looked how I felt. Miserable.

"Unpacking pots." I wasn't in the mood for small talk. In fact, I wasn't in the mood to talk to him period. A new form of rage simmered within, and I was unsure of what I would say if I started talking.

"Listen, I know you're angry with me. What did you expect me to do?"

"I don't expect anything from you. But Seri does. She expects you to understand her, and you have no clue." Oh, Lord. I was going to say something I was going to regret, yet I was powerless to stop. "Have you ever wondered why Seri struggles so much? Have you ever put thought into what she is suffering with every day?" He was uncomfortable with this conversation, but it needed to be had.

"How can I think of anything else? You constantly bring it up. Every. Single. Damn. Day. That's all you talk about. That's all you seem capable to think about!"

His words stung. I had a feeling everything we were about to say to each other was going to pack a punch. "One of us has to! She isn't a typical kid! She doesn't think like us, she doesn't act like us, and she sure as shit doesn't handle things like we do. She needed help, and we laughed it off. That eats at me. Every day I wonder why we didn't listen to Dr. Coldbrooke. And when I try to bring it up with you, you shut me down instantly. Why?"

"Dammit, Addie. Not this shit again. Every kid has different quirks and feelings. The problem is you smother her to death! You don't allow her to process anything. You practically chew her food, and all she has to do is swallow! I don't see you catering to Ivy like this. In fact, I don't see you doing much with Ivy at all."

He had never spoken to me like this. Not in all the years we had been married. Our emotions were bubbling over like my boiling chow sometimes did, splattering the stove top with ugly words that could never be unsaid.

"Don't bring Ivy into this. She knows I love her." Yet as I said this, the accuracy of his words landed on my heart.

"How does she know? When do you find the time to tell her? When Seri is sleeping? Cause every other minute, you are stuck to Seri's hip or thinking of when you will be stuck to her hip again."

Wow. Was this really what he thought of me? Resentment oozed out of him.

"What would you like me to do, Dex? Pretend our daughter isn't struggling? When I hear her crying at night, do I tell her to stop her whining? When she gets worked up and can't breathe, do I tell her to suck it up and act like an adult? When she is paralyzed with fear, do I give her a shove and tell her to get moving? Push her head under in a public pool until she gets over her fear of germs or drowns?"

I was almost hysterical now. "I seem to recall you giving her tough love constantly. How has that worked out for ya? For her? How was your big talk at the store that night she quit AAA? You can't discipline this out of her or wish it away. Take today as a perfect example. You couldn't see her anxiety level at maximum capacity before you shoved her onto the ice. That your idea of a success story?"

I slammed a pot so hard onto a shelf, it shattered. My heart felt like it was doing the same. I kicked the empty box to the side and ran my hands through my hair.

"Oh, I see. It's my fault Seri tripped today. I must have been hoping she would fail, huh?" He was worked up and speaking louder with each sentence. "How am I the bad guy for believing in our daughter today? How is it my fault she can't handle most situations she is in? This is just fucking fantastic. You smother her to death, yet I'm the asshole for trying to push her to be her own person. Look in the mirror, Addie. You'll see who the problem is."

"Do you think I don't know I am failing our daughter? That I am responsible for how far down the rabbit hole she has gone? My God, don't you see that Seri's struggles are killing me?" Rage gave way to raw grief. His words were cutting my heart to shreds. I needed to sit down. I felt light-headed to the point I was dizzy. My legs were about to give out. I grabbed the stool in front of the counter and clunked down onto the hard plastic. Dexter seemed to regret some of what he had said and lowered his voice.

"Addie, I didn't come here to blame you. I just think you over dramatize every event in her life, and it makes it a bigger deal than it needs to be. Pass today off like it was nothing, and she will too."

He stepped closer, but I raised my hand to stop him. What a ridiculous thing for him to say. When had Seri passed off anything that happened in her life as nothing? He knew this. He just wasn't willing to admit it. "Don't. Don't come near me. Not when you refuse to see what is happening right under your nose."

He stopped.

"Today is the least of our worries. She won't even apply to university with a ninety-eight average. She's scared to death she won't be accepted. She has one true friend and shies away from people because she doesn't feel worthy. She cries almost every night, and I can't for the life me figure out why! Now you ask me to pass another day off like it was nothing? When will you see she needs more than we have been able to give her?"

"Fine. Blame me if it makes you feel better. What's more distance between us?" He turned on his heels and headed for the door.

"So, that's your solution? To walk out on another conversation? To wish this all away, blame me for sucking as a parent and hope that everything will magically, mystically work itself out?"

When he turned to face me, the sadness I felt was mirrored in his eyes. "What does talking help, Addie? Is this constructive? Are we getting anywhere?"

He had a point. This conversation had been a disaster. "No. But it's time we take Seri to a professional who can help her. She has something going on that's beyond us. I'm tired of pretending there isn't something seriously wrong." I stood, steadied myself and wiped at my face with the sleeves of my sweater.

"Fine. You want her to talk to someone, then by all means sign her up. But my daughter isn't crazy." His voiced cracked.

There it was. The root of his anger. He was afraid for Seri and what we may find out. He was afraid she would be labelled crazy. The stigma of mental illness wound tightly in his soul.

"She isn't crazy. She's lost. She's lost in her thoughts, stuck in her own mind, and we need to find her again. I want our daughter back."

He stepped forward, seemed to think better of it and turned to leave. He paused long enough I thought he would speak, but he quietly walked out of the store. After I heard the door close, I collapsed onto the stool and held my head in my hands.

Marriage had been my safe haven. Dex had always been there for me when I needed him throughout our marriage. Until now. It was beginning to feel like a prison. I felt isolated and alone. Not only did I feel like a bad mother to Seri, but Dexter's insights had me feeling less than a shit hot wife or a good mom to Ivy. Didn't he understand me? I thought he grasped the fact that the distance between us wasn't intentional. I had to give Seri my attention until I figured out how to make her happy. I loved Ivy every bit as much as I did Seri and was insulted he thought otherwise. Ivy knew how much I loved her. She didn't need me the way Seri did.

He and I loved Seri. We both wanted what was best for her. We had different styles of parenting but sadly, neither approach was working. It was painfully clear it was time for something different. It was time to get Seri professional help before it was too late. If the cost was my marriage, it was a price I was willing to pay.

March 24th, 2018

Dexter

Spring wasn't my favourite time of year. Especially at work. The ground was beginning to thaw, and there was constant rain. That meant treading through mud at the construction site. The project on for today was pouring footing for a garage and at one point, my boot had gotten stuck in the mud. Normally little things like that didn't bother me, but I was easily incensed with most things the last few weeks. It was because of Addie. Or was it Seri? It was hard to tell anymore. Addie and I had hardly spoken since our fight in the shop three weeks ago. We had nothing to say. I didn't know how to retract what I had said, and it was hard to bounce back from hurtful words. We both had said things we didn't regret necessarily, and that was a hard pill to swallow. It was easier to apologize when I hadn't meant what I'd said, but impossible when I had spoken the truth. How did I move forward from that?

We were now at odds about Seri getting a job. Addie was concerned, but I thought she needed to look for work. I broached the subject last week. Seri needed to start saving money and to have something to do that didn't involve being home. Since the championship game, Seri had withdrawn into herself even more. She had nothing but school to keep her mind occupied. Her routine consisted of coming home, doing homework if she had any and then retreating to her room to watch TV. She had no interest in hanging out with Mari, and she napped like it was a profession. On the weekends, she snuggled under a blanket on the couch, sound asleep less than two or three hours after getting out of bed and eating breakfast. I didn't get the same amount of sleep in a week Seri banked in a day. I would've said something, but Addie's words kept ringing in my ears. "How is your tough love working out?" Not too damn good, was the answer.

"Cement truck should be here in a few minutes, Dex." Ivan's voice broke through my thoughts.

"Okay. Let's get these last three panels up."

Ivan hopped down to help with the task at hand. Ivan was a great worker and had been working with me for the past year. I had hired him straight out of community college. As a recently-graduated carpenter, he had taught this old dog a few new tricks of the construction trade. He was young, only twenty-two, and his youth I envied. He was single and carefree, and there were times I wished I could trade him places.

For the next two hours, I thought only of work. The garage we were building was going up quickly. I loved when projects went together smoothly. Muddy boots aside, work did for me what sleep did for Seri. It was an escape from things I didn't want to deal with. I found myself working later and later each day and even started working the occasional weekend, which I had said I would never do with a family.

But the thoughts of going home, especially tonight, was not a happy thought. I didn't want to feel the tension when I walked through the door. I hated how awkward things had gotten with Addie. I didn't want to go home and talk to Seri about work. After much persuasion, she had started a new job on Monday, and it was not going well. The first night she came home, she went straight to her room and sobbed her heart out. I heard her through the closed door. She cried the next two nights as well. Adalynn had spoken with her the third night without much success. She told Seri she had no choice but to keep working and that with each passing day, this new routine would get easier for her. She held Seri while she cried herself to sleep, and it was hard for me to watch. I had to give Addie credit. She was doing all she could to have this work out for Seri. Normally, she'd have backed down by now, but she was holding her ground. She told Seri she would drive her to and from work, if she wanted the company, stop in and have break with her or even talk to her boss to explain this wasn't easy for her. But Seri was having none of it. She didn't want to co-operate. She wanted to quit and stay home.

Seri was on the list to see a therapist. Adalynn had called the day after our blow up and was told Seri would be placed on a waiting list. I had no idea there was a waiting list for such a thing. Not only was there a list, but it would be six to eight months before she could get in to see someone. The thought of that many people needing help with their mental health was staggering. I had thought when Addie made the call, all this would be dealt with and behind us by now. Seri still didn't even have an appointment.

The rest of the day passed in a blur. My thoughts alternated between work and Seri, and I was struck by the irony of how I was now doing what I had accused Addie of: constantly dwelling on Seri and her well-being.

One wet foot, a garage footing and two jobs priced-up later, I headed home. When I arrived, I was surprised to see Ivy alone in the front yard. I hopped out of the truck and walked towards her. "Hey, Ives, what's up?" The closer I got, the easier it was to see she was agitated.

"Oh, you know, the usual. Mom is in the house trying to calm Seri down. She refuses to go to work. I was tired of listening to them, so I came out here to tinker around." She held up the axe she was carrying.

"Going to chop down the forest?" I tried to be funny. Humour was not my strong suit. That was Ivy's forte.

"Actually, yeah. I'm attempting to make a mountain bike trail through the woods."

"Great idea. Need some help?" I wanted the distraction. I had no desire to go into the house. Plus it would be nice to hang with Ivy. I hadn't had much time with her lately. At the rate the girls were growing up, spending any kind of time with them was soon going to be a thing of the past. They'd have their own lives before I knew it.

"Naw. I think Mom needs back up. She was near tears." With that, Ivy headed towards the woods.

"Well, be careful. That axe isn't a toy." She waved the axe in the air as a sign she had heard me and disappeared into the woods.

I turned and faced the house. Dread shot through my body but the sooner I faced this, the faster it would be over. I heard Addie and Seri before I saw them. Addie, who was usually patient, was unravelling.

"Fifteen minutes, Seri. We have 15 minutes to get you to work! You're not losing this battle. Now go get ready!"

I walked in and saw Seri on the couch, crying into a pillow on her lap and Addie standing over her, on the verge of her own breakdown.

"What's going on?" I hoped my innocent question would defuse the tension.

"Seri doesn't want to go to work." Addie didn't look at me. She stared at Seri, willing her to move.

"Seri, what's the issue at work? Why is it so hard to go?" I was surprised at how calm I sounded when I felt like smashing something out of pure frustration.

When she looked at me, my mouth gaped. Fighting to steal away from the horror in her blood-shot eyes, I stared at her hands clutched so tightly beneath her chin, a crowbar couldn't pry them apart. The skin on her hands was chaffed, and her raw knuckles where blood had dried in cracks were turning various shades of pink from tears diluting the blood. Her hunched position resembled that of a frozen child on a winter sidewalk with no coat to keep them warm. Who was she? What had provoked this reaction? A job? Leaving the house? This made no sense.

Why had I never seen this before? What kind of father was I to force this kind of hysteria onto my own daughter? Until she had therapy, I was not forcing her to do anything that made her feel this uncomfortable. I was fully on board with getting her professional help. I closed my mouth, swallowed to calm my nerves, then took a deep breath, hoping to disguise my fear and resolve this without further conflict.

"You know what, Seri, let's not worry about work. Call them and explain it's too much for you right now, and just relax, okay?"

The relief on Seri's face made me feel like I had done the right thing for the first time in a long time for her. This was likely what Addie wanted too. She always let Seri do the easier thing instead of pushing her but when I looked at Addie for support, she looked furious. What the hell was going on? Why did Adalynn look like she wanted to kick me down a flight of stairs?

Seri jumped off the couch and grabbed me in a hug. "Thanks for understanding, Daddy." She hadn't called me daddy in years. "I'll call work."

When Seri left the room, I tried to gauge Addie's mood. She had taken a seat where Seri had been sitting. She picked up the pillow that was wet from tears and stared at it like it had the answers we desperately needed.

"You all right with that decision, Adalynn?" I hadn't called her Adalynn in years. She had always been Addie to me. My Addie. Adalynn felt so formal coming out of my mouth, but it was fitting considering where we were in our marriage. We were fast becoming strangers.

"Does it matter? I can't undo it now."

Nothing about my life should surprise me anymore, but I was not expecting this to cause another rift between us. If anything, I thought it would ease tension.

Adalynn had been the one to shield Seri when things got rough and do all she could to keep her from having panic attacks. After looking at Seri sitting there in her world of terror, I finally understood the desire to protect her. I assumed Addie appreciated that.

"I don't get it. First you accuse me of pushing too hard and now that I have backed off, I'm still handling this wrong?" I hated the sound of my voice. It was rude, and the last person I wanted to be rude to was the woman I loved more than anything.

Addie rose to face me. She seemed to be thinking of what she wanted to say. "I never said you were wrong. I haven't said anything at all." She pushed past me and went into the kitchen.

I followed. I was not dropping this conversation. "Well, you haven't been speechless since I met you." Not constructive words, but I didn't know how else to relieve the anger I was feeling.

"Fine. You want my thoughts? I think you just set her back again. I think she could have gotten over this if we had pushed her a few more days. Maybe you were right saying I babied her too much." Her tone suggested she was not buying a word she was saying.

"Really? You never pushed her to do shit before. Why now?" All too familiar with anger brewing at the surface, I tried to stay calm. "Can't you be happy I am finally on the same page as you?"

She looked at me and laughed a joyless laugh. "Same page? We haven't been on the same page for months, Dexter. We aren't even in the same bed most nights." Now it was Adalynn who was being formal. "I have replayed our fight over and over and keep hearing your words on repeat in my mind, and I don't feel good about it. Mostly because I don't think you were wrong. That's hard to admit." She turned and held onto the countertop for support.

"I never did push Seri. I was scared to! It broke my heart to see her panic in new situations. It still does." She turned to face me. "You looked at her today and for the first time, you saw the agony in her face that I have seen for years. You were oblivious to it because you didn't want to see it." She paused long enough to regain her crumbling composure. "But I have seen it. For years. And I did nothing. I kept making excuses for her."

She lost the battle and cried for the second time today. I wanted to go to her, but I didn't want her to push me away like she did the last time we had fought. It hurt like hell when she rejected me. There was so much I wanted to say, but it was Adalynn who spoke.

"Why couldn't we talk to each other about this? Why did it take this long for us to see that Seri isn't okay?"

I had no answer. I knew what my shortcomings were, but I had no confessions to share with her right now. How was I supposed to see something I didn't want to see? How did I fix something I wouldn't admit was broken? I wanted to share my thoughts to ease her burden of guilt. She wasn't the only one who had fallen short. I just couldn't voice any of it. "I don't know what to say. Isn't it enough we are on the same page right now?"

"Are we? Cause I don't ever remember feeling so far apart from you."

We stood stuck in time. Neither of us offered up any comfort. No shoulder given for the other to cry on. The safety net our love used to provide was missing. I didn't like talking about emotions but felt if I didn't say something, I may not get the chance again.

"Adalynn, I..." No more words would pass through my lips. Try as I might, I couldn't own up to my failings. I had no love to offer her. We stood silently for another minute, then she walked out of the kitchen and what felt like, out of my life.

Seraphina

"What's your problem, Seri? We got out of work. Why are you so down?"

Stop! I screamed at The Voice. Please, let me sleep.

I had been trying to sleep for more than four hours, but to no avail. Laying in my double bed with only my thoughts as company, I was reliving this afternoon. Dad was the one who had finally relented and told me I didn't have to go to work. After the brief feeling of relief of staying home, the sensation that I had failed, set in. How could I possibly be feeling worse for getting what I wanted? That was the real problem. I wanted to work. I wanted to play hockey. Oh, how I wanted to see my friends. It was The Voice who wanted me all to itself. It was The Voice who was never happy.

"That's not true, Seri! I am giving you the truth. Sometimes the truth hurts. You did everyone a favour by staying home. You can't fail at home."

I wiped my cheeks and was not surprised with the amount of moisture that had accumulated. For four hellish days, I had been crying on and off. I was powerless to stop the barrage of tears. This morning, after days of unrelenting weeping, Dad had made an empty threat to give me something to cry about, and not even that had worked. The beast in my head was out for blood. I sensed it. I felt it. I had no control of my own thoughts, and the direness of the situation was taking a serious toll. No matter what decision I made, The Voice was unsatisfied. When Dad had relented and told me I didn't have to go to work, I was stunned.

First, pure joy had invaded my thoughts, but it quickly gave way to the feeling I had failed yet again. Mom was not on board with the idea. After I had gotten off the phone with work, I headed to the kitchen to get a drink, and I heard Mom and Dad talking. They were fighting over me. Again. The memory worked up my nerves.

"Life is hard for them with your problems, Seri."

Deep breaths in and out were not working, and a huge part of me didn't know if my mind was telling me the truth or not. Was I the reason my parents' marriage was crumbling? I didn't need The Voice to answer to know the truth.

Scared the evil part of my mind would lead me to a point of no return, I hid my face in my pillow and tried to fill my mind with positive thoughts. Nothing. The only voice I heard, oddly, was my own, repeating words and phrases I didn't want to hear. I couldn't break the cycle or overpower my inner thoughts. I hadn't been able to for years, and those years had finally caught up to me tonight. My remaining strength faded, and I surrendered completely.

"Are you finally seeing things clearly, Seri? Do you see the damage you've done? How hard this world really is?"

My chest tightened. Air felt less and less effective with each breath. What was wrong with me? I pleaded with myself. Why am I like this?

"Because you're not worthy. We've been over this. Your family is tired of the drama. You're a lot to take. Don't you see your parents' marriage crumbling? Who do you think they blame for that? You hear them fight. You heard them tonight. It's always about you."

The truth of that statement pierced my heart. I saw the strain in their marriage. Dad had been coming home later and later, and I saw how sad Mom was when she didn't think anyone was watching her. I was destroying the two people I loved more than life itself.

"You think I don't know that?" I hissed, this time out loud to the empty room. "Do you think I don't know I should just end things and take away the burden from my family? I see the toll it takes on everyone near me."

My outburst didn't settle the beast that occupied the whole of my mind. It had set up camp, the biggest it had ever pitched, and it had no intentions of leaving until it got the result it wanted.

"First clear thought you've had, Seri. A thought, I can get on board with. Did you see your mom crying tonight in the garden when she thought no one was watching? That was your doing. You know your dad hates coming home. He has never worked this much in his life. You pushed him to that because your mother can't think of anyone but you. And poor Ivy. The girl might as well be an orphan."

At that moment, I saw things as clear as I have ever allowed myself to see them. I saw myself through The Voice's eyes... my eyes. Flashbacks shot through my mind like an old black and white film.

Vividly, I saw the pain and sheer disappointment in my mother's eyes after I had quit work tonight. I heard Dad telling Mom in a moment of rage, he hated coming home. I saw the fight Ivy and I had a few months ago, and she was telling me I was a bitch who thought of no one but myself. Her crying had woken me on many nights, and I heard her prayers for Mom to go to her and ask what was wrong. I felt germs on my hands taunting me, and the need to scrub away those germs seared in my brain. The devastation of losing our last championship game because of my carelessness echoed in my head like a slap shot in an empty rink. The blank applications hidden in my nightstand drawer jabbed like nails into my skin. Applying to a university meant another rejection. I wasn't good enough to attend. The weight of everything flashing before my eyes like the last seconds of a lost game was too much. I was mentally collapsing.

I lifted my head from the pillow and saw it was a little past 3:00 am. A new wave of despair washed over me. My thoughts were too loud, too overbearing. It was all starting to make sense. Wouldn't it be easier to end things? If I did, everyone could go on with their days and not worry about me and what havoc my problems would cause. Wouldn't this bring Mom and Dad together? Make Ivy feel wanted again?

"Yes, that's it, Seri. Think logically. Think of your loved ones..." The Voice was a mesmerizing whisper, sweet and encouraging. "You will find the peace you've been searching for, Seraphina. No more crazy thoughts to worry about. Only a place to rest your weary soul. You'll be with God. There is no sadness in heaven."

Heaven. I had heard about heaven every Sunday in church for years. No sadness or tears in heaven. Only peace and love.

Defeated, drained physically, emotionally and mentally, I stumbled to the kitchen. Step by step, I knew my feet were moving, but it didn't seem like I was the one in control of them. I had let The Voice take control of not just my mind, but my body too. I didn't flip the light switch as I entered the kitchen. Instead I followed the path my feet had taken for the last 16 years of my life and walked to the drawer beside the sink.

"The utensil drawer, Seri. A steak knife should do."

I did not argue. I was unable to think for myself. I obediently did what was asked of me. The light over the stove dimly lit the kitchen, but I was not able to see through the tears I was crying. I gently felt my way around the drawer, ever so careful as my fingers moved over the blades of the different knives. My hand felt the cool steel of the steak knife, and I slid my hand to the handle. A random thought popped into my head. Someone had used that knife at supper for a totally different reason, and I had dried and placed it in the drawer only a few short hours ago. Would my family enjoy steak again after...?

"Focus..., Seri... Let's finish what you need to do."

The Voice still held its power over me, so I picked up the knife, turned my back to the cupboards and slid all the way down to the floor, the knife falling beside me.

"How did I get here?" I asked myself, not knowing if I wanted to hear the answer. Trying with all my might, I had to find the quiet strength Mom told me I possessed.

"That's not important now, Seri. What matters is you can make the pain for you and your family go away. You can find the peace you have been wanting for so long."

I gathered my last bit of strength and tried to reason with The Voice one more time. "But won't they be sad when I'm gone? Don't I have anything to offer this world?"

"They will hurt but only for a bit, Seri... They know why you need to do this. They see you suffering. Your family suffers too, but they will be okay. They have only ever wanted you to be happy. You can be happy now, Seri. You tried here and have nothing left to give. It's easier for all of us if you do this. Trust me. I wouldn't lie to you."

My last bit of resistance slipped away. My head fell into my arms that were resting on my knees, and sobs wracked my body. A final, tragic and inaccurate account of my life was being shown again in my mind. All the times I had wanted to call friends to hang out but knew they wouldn't want to. All the times I backed out of tryouts because I was no good. The marks below eighty even though I had studied. The disappointment in my parents' eyes. The disgust in my sister's face. The shame in my heart for who I was. It was too much for my soul and mind to bear.

I gingerly laid my left wrist upright on my knee and picked up the knife with my other hand. I felt the touch of the cold blade on my skin and curiously wondered what the pain was going to feel like.

"Do it. You're almost there." The Voice was soothing, like a lullaby. "Hush, little Seri, don't you cry..."

The slice was fast and surprisingly less painful than I had anticipated. The blood spurted before the blade was done making its remarkably straight line. Quickly and robotically, I switched the knife to my rapidly-weakening hand and sliced the other wrist with faster and deeper precision. The knife clattered to the floor, bouncing away like an unwilling accomplice.

I slumped farther and farther down onto vinyl flooring that slowly changed from its original cream color to crimson red. I had nothing to do but wait. My energy drained, and sleep beckoned. A deep sleepiness I had begged for earlier that night descended on me.

It was in that precise moment, I realized nothing was running through my mind. There were no whispers, no dreadful stories of the terrible person I was. The Voice was gone. For the first time that I could remember, I heard nothing. I smiled as my eyes closed. There was only silence. Pure, still, peaceful, welcoming silence. Peace. The Voice had been right. I finally had peace. We would all finally have peace. That was the last thought I had before my world went black.

July 20th, 2018

Adalynn

The day started like every other day this summer: hot, sticky and barely a breeze worth mentioning. The high-pitched hum of the air conditioner in the bedroom window wasn't as relieving a sound as one would have hoped. It was struggling desperately, constantly straining and shifting gears to keep up to the sun's relentless power. I slowly sat up in bed, getting ready to brave the day's heat and careful not to disturb Dex while he slept. He slept downstairs most nights, but the air conditioning was a temptation he couldn't resist on hot nights. He didn't have to get up for another hour or so to head to work. Odd that he worked so many Saturdays now given all we'd been through, but he was happiest when he was working, so I didn't say much about it.

As much as I hated the summer heat, I could escape into the house or my shop when it got too hot, while Dex had to battle it all day at work. The heat was getting to him lately. He was never happy when he returned home after a long day. He used to talk passionately about the projects he took on, sometimes taking me for drive-bys to see the work he had completed.

Now I was lucky to know what project he was working on. In fairness, I never asked anymore. Not that I didn't want to hear about his day because I did. We just didn't know how to talk to one another.

I wanted to go back in time. Before Seri started hearing the voice in her mind, and before our lives had flipped upside down on that horrendous night four months ago. I longed for the days when Dexter sneaked up behind me if I was alone in the house when he got home from work. Closing my eyes, I remembered him putting his filthy hands on me, rubbing me all over, kissing my neck and telling me I had no choice but to enjoy a hot shower with him because I was now a dirty mess like him. I would put up a pretend fight, then stop whatever I was doing and let him lead me by the hand into the bathroom. My skin tingled thinking of the hot steam filling the bathroom as we made our desire for one another clear. It used to be my favourite time of day. Not only for the afternoon nooky, but because we shared stories of how our day had been. He was my best friend, and I loved telling him my day's highs and lows, and I loved watching him light up with pride when telling me about his latest project.

Nowadays, he came home, sweat dripping off him, with little to no energy left for anything or anyone. No more work stories, no more drives to check out his projects, and certainly no hot showers together. I was lucky if he glanced in my direction.

I wished I could blame the heat for the distance that had crept between us this last year, but I knew it was much deeper than fatigue from the sun. It was way less painful to pretend he was too tired to be with me than to face a different and more stark reality that things had irrevocably shifted in our twenty-one-year marriage. With these thoughts tumbling around in my head, I undressed as stealthily as I could to avoid any awkwardness between Dexter and me. Another part of me wanted him to wake up. I remembered a time when mornings brought both of us pleasure, the way he would slide his hand across my body, under my nightie, slightly and purposefully brushing my bare nipple as he leaned in and pulled me tightly to him. The way he whispered his good mornings into my ear, and how quickly and easily he aroused me. I loved feeling his breath on my skin, hearing him whisper he wanted me.

I turned my head and peered down at his handsome bearded face and thought about reaching for a kiss. To run my fingers through his beard. He hadn't attempted so much as a kiss the last seven months. One night last week, I tried to put myself out there, sucked up my pride to bridge the enormous gap that had formed between us. I dug out his favourite negligee, walked into our room where he had been watching TV, and slowly sauntered in front of the screen to the window and glanced out. I stood there for a bit, bending over slightly, leaning on the window ledge, a little show for him, but he was only interested in the regularly scheduled program. I was embarrassed he hadn't picked up the subtle hint, and total humiliation had set in when I sat in bed beside him, and he rolled over and feigned sleep.

With this memory fresh in my mind, I abruptly stopped midway to kiss him and fought hard against my desire for him. The feeling of rejection replaced the memory of his touch. I swallowed the lump that had risen in my throat. It was much too early and way too easy to fall prey to my never ending thoughts. Now was not the time to wallow in my self-pity. Or the hardships that had befallen our marriage. Not with what our daughter was dealing with. My focus had to be on her needs.

The laminate floor was warm under my feet as I made the two short steps to the dresser. Sliding off the rest of my night attire, I stood naked, looking for a tank top to put on, knowing I needed as little clothing today as possible. Light slowly filtered through the cracks between the curtains, giving enough brightness to find my outfit with ease. As I climbed into shorts that matched my blue tank top, I wondered when our summers started getting so blessed hot.

I yanked my hair into a black ponytail elastic and headed into the hall where Seraphina's room stood before me. The room had originally been Ivy's and technically still was. We asked Ivy to switch rooms after Seri had come home from the hospital so I could hear her at night. I lived in constant fear I may not hear Seri if she got up, and it was easier to relax with her directly across the hall than at the end where Ivy now was. Ivy had no issues with giving up her room, and I was more grateful than she would ever know. She had recently mentioned wanting to return to her room, but I wasn't ready to make the switch. It was no big deal one way or the other for anyone other than me.

Seri had the door closed, not only at night but most days. Emotions so raw and powerful washed over me, almost making me nauseous. Staring at the barrier that stood between us, I repeated to myself, she's okay, she's okay, until the sharp panic subsided. The sadness that reached my heart when I touched the door handle was immense, almost paralyzing.

Four months had drifted past in a blur, and my emotions were not in check. Fighting the urge to go in and check on my daughter was futile. I slowly, quietly turned the knob to gaze in without being detected, holding my breath when the knob turned fully and the latch made its springy noise as it was drawn back. Her night light was shining, even though the cracks of sunlight dominated the room's light. I edged closer to the foot of her bed. Her silhouette danced in the soft glow of morning light. She seemed peaceful at this moment. Free from her thoughts and worries. A stark contrast from the night she had tried to take her life.

Still a bit too far away from the bed and desperate to see the rise and fall of her sheet, I edged closer and held my breath. The sheet moved upward, paused and then receded down. Again. Upward, paused and receded. I watched the trio of movements for a moment until I breathed again. I felt like a new mother watching over her firstborn infant.

Satisfied, if only for this fleeting moment, I retreated from the room as quietly as I had entered and sighed with relief when the door securely shut.

Another night had passed. We had another day to show her what she meant to the world. I continued the trek down the hall and quickly came to the next door: Ivy's room. Thinking of Ivy brought a smile to my face. Her quick wit was both amusing and frustrating, depending on the situation. Lately she was faster to anger, but what teenager didn't know more than their parents? We had all changed in the past few months, so I didn't worry too much about her mood swings. We had healing to do, and anger was part of the process.

The tension that had set at the moment I had opened my eyes, eased. It was a relief that I didn't have to peer in or check on Ivy. She didn't need me in her space, and I didn't feel it necessary to be in it. My footsteps didn't slow as I walked past her room and headed into the kitchen. I had no doubt she was sleeping and most likely wouldn't emerge from her room until hunger forced her out.

My time with Ivy these past four months was almost non-existent. I loved both my girls with all my heart and equally, but my attention was never able to rest solely on Ivy when we were together. Too many of my days were consumed with Seraphina and the awful night I had found her in the kitchen. I couldn't figure out how to get past the traumatic event, and I wasn't sure I ever would. Therapy had been intense, and Seri was doing amazingly well, learning how to deal with her anxiety and OCD, but I couldn't wrap my head around the fact I had been unable to help my little girl when she had needed me the most. I had failed her so deeply. No matter how many times the therapist reassured Dex and me that we had done everything we could for Seri, it never eased my guilt. I was her mom. I should have known Seri was at her breaking point. How could I have not provided what she needed?

Now that Seri understood what OCD was and they had put a name to the voice in her head, she seemed happier and more in control of her thoughts than ever before.

Strangely, her brush with death had given her a heightened sense of how important living was. The clarity therapy had given her was amazing. Her smile reached her eyes now and although life hadn't magically changed, she was becoming a different person, which I was extremely grateful for. It was me who was still lost. Dex, Ivy and I had to attend our own private therapy sessions, and that was not going smoothly for me. Dex was getting more out of it than I was. He understood Seri needed to do most of the work on her own but to me, I didn't know how to let her handle this on her own. I was scared to take a step back. The therapist kept telling me to put faith in Seri by giving her more space and to trust the work she was putting in. I wanted to give her that. I honestly did, but it was hard. I smothered her more now than I ever had. She told me to focus on Ivy because she needed me too. I wanted to ask if Ivy had mentioned that during a therapy session, but she couldn't tell me what Ivy had said. It was confidential. I was sure Ivy knew how much I loved her, but a few extra moments with her each day may be what both of us needed.

I made a mental note that someday soon, Ivy and I would have our own day. We would hop into the car and go wherever she wished to go. She had just gotten her driver's licence and loved to drive. Once I felt comfortable leaving her sister home alone, we would paint the town whatever colour she wanted. Perhaps this afternoon was as good a day as any to start living and putting my fears aside. If Ivy was interested, we could take a drive, roll the windows down, crank the tunes and enjoy the afternoon together. I would propose the idea only after assessing Seri's emotional state to determine if it was okay to leave her alone.

Breathing deeply, I stepped into the kitchen. This was another hard thing for me: stepping into this room. Looking toward the sink made me physically shake, even now, months later. The smell of blood lingered, though I had scrubbed the floor with every cleaner in the house, including bleach. No matter how many times I washed it, the odour from the blood around Seri's body triggered my nose. I had worked my hands until they were raw, bleeding and cracked, and still the smell struck me when I entered the room. I sensed the horror of seeing my baby girl lying in front of me, barely breathing. I still felt the blood oozing between my fingers as I fought to hold her wounds together until the ambulance had gotten there. It was only by the grace of God, I had gotten to her on time. I had woken in a lather of sweat and a sense that something was seriously wrong. It was like God had taken me by the hand and led me straight into the kitchen, where my worst nightmare had become a reality. I am convinced He knew I couldn't live without my daughter and helped me save her life that night.

I was allowed to stay with Seri at the hospital until she was stabilized, then I was sent home. We weren't allowed to see her during her two days of evaluation, and we received only a progress call each morning. Once I had returned to the hospital on day three, Dex had gone to work transforming the kitchen without telling me. I had given serious thought to moving to a new home that first week, but when I closed my eyes, it didn't matter where I was, the image of Seri's lifeless body was as vivid as I had seen it on that dreadful night. I had held off mentioning it to Dex, but he must have felt the same way because the transformation before me was extensive.

When Seri and I had returned home nine days later, the kitchen looked completely different. The floor had been retiled in rich brown colours, and the cupboards had been sanded down and painted two different tones of brown. A beautiful, small kitchen island had been added so when I walked into the room, the spot where Seri had been lying wasn't the first place I saw. It had been a tremendous amount of work in a short time, but I suspect it was how Dex wanted to help in the recovery. Changing the room in appearance so it would be easier to enter, had been a thoughtful gesture. It was also something constructive for him to do while dealing with what had happened. When we had returned home, the difference in the kitchen had been a welcomed change. I never told him, but I was immensely grateful. I wasn't sure I would have been able to stay in our home if he hadn't put in all that work.

I opened the fridge door and quickly chose breakfast. Yogurt and orange juice was fast and easy, and I guzzled it up in less than five minutes. Tossing the yogurt container away and dumping the last mouthful of orange juice down the sink, I slipped on my garden boots and slid the patio door open. Stepping onto the deck, the wall of humidity was palpable, but not yet overwhelming. I estimated three hours in the garden before I was chased back inside by the sun. Maybe getting ice cream would be something Ivy and I could do on our drive, or maybe a trip to the beach for a swim.

I surveyed my thriving garden, took in the sight of my shop at the opposite end of our property, and smiled at the task at hand. It was the end of August, and most plants were at their peak. The raspberry patch was always the first thing to catch my eye. Beautiful, six foot-tall vines with specks of red throughout the green foliage as the berries began to ripen. Tomatoes were in abundance, cascading over their cages, glorious in all their shades of red. I couldn't wait to get the salsa on the go and fill the shelves at the shop. I had even nicknamed one part of my garden "the Salsa Corner" for the onions, peppers and tomatoes that were planted solely with that purpose in mind. With my heart a little lighter, I grabbed the wheelbarrow, trowel and weeder and headed to the first part of the garden. An hour or two of working the land with my hands would give me a sense of accomplishment and pleasure, rare feelings for me these days, and I was deeply looking forward to them filling my heavy, tired soul.

Ivy

Four months. That's how long it had been. Four months since my family had drastically changed. Why I thought this would be the morning Mom would pause at my door, open it and check in on me, I would never know. I heard her tiptoe out of Seri's room, close the door quietly and then, like every single morning for the past four months, hell, more like years, briskly shuffled past my room without so much as a thought of coming in to check on me or of any thought of me at all.

For the first few months after Seri's suicide attempt, I totally understood Mom's need to reassure herself that Seri was okay. I even checked on Seri. It was tough to sleep at night wondering what she was dealing with in her mind. The shock of that dreadful night was as fresh as if it had happened yesterday. The sound of Mom's gut-wrenching scream, racing to the kitchen and seeing her trying to will Seri back to life, trying with all her might to literally hold my sister together, hearing the ambulance's sirens and watching the lights fade as they whisked Seri off to an unknown fate, is a night I would never forget for as long as I lived. Dad had scooped me up with one arm, ushered me back to my room and told me not to come out until he said it was ok.

I had crept to the kitchen when I no longer heard the sirens, and what I saw was almost as bad as seeing Seri lifeless. Dad was on the floor with a mountain of paper towel, trying to soak up the blood. There was so much blood. It was on the floor, Dad's pajama pants, the cupboard doors. Wallowing in tears, he hadn't seen me watching. Inconsolable sobs racked his body. I had never seen my dad cry. Ever. It was too much for me to bear witness to.

Quietly, I had returned to my room on unsteady legs and did the only thing I could think of that night. I prayed. I asked God to bring Seri back to us. I had never spoken to anyone about that night. Not to Mom or Dad. Not even to the therapist I was made to see. I've done all I can to block that night out of my memory, but I still had vivid nightmares that woke me. Two different nightmares kept reoccurring. In one, Seri was drowning in a pool of blood while I watched, laughing from the side of the pool while I sunbathed. I laughed and told her she was so dramatic, and I taunted her as she gasped for air. I think this was how my guilt manifested itself in my subconscious. I hated that I had used the word *crazy* with Seri. It was a heavy cross I would bear forever.

The other nightmare had me trying to stop the blood coming from Seri's wrists. I tried hard to apply pressure, but it was never enough. The blood kept rising until it was drowning me. The second nightmare was directly related to the scene that unfolded that night in the kitchen. As hard as Mom tried, the blood refused to stop seeping past the cloth barrier she had tied around the wounds. I couldn't unsee that no matter how I tried.

The nightmares seemed real and when I woke from them, I couldn't stop shaking. I wanted to share these with Mom, have her wrap her arms around me and tell me everything was going to be okay, but I couldn't. A part of me didn't want to add to her already overflowing plate. Another part of me didn't want to feel the rejection or indifference that might follow if I shared my deepest thoughts and feelings with her. The demand of Seri's problems always made mine look small. It was hard not to agree that I should suck up my problems and wear my big girl drawers after what had taken place.

I sometimes felt guilty for ever needing Mom or wanting her attention, but I desperately wanted my mom back. To laugh with, talk to and be cherished by. It wasn't on purpose, she was neglecting me. She was doing the best she knew how. I thought at some point though, she would miss me in some capacity. That she would let her worries go for a day and spend it with me. Sadly, that was not yet the case.

Mom had known for a long time that Seri needed help. She just couldn't figure out what kind of help that was. She had no clue Seri was hearing a voice in her mind, and I know that guilt weighed heavy on her, and Dad too. Therapy did wonders for Seri, but it was having the opposite effect on Mom. I think for Seri, the biggest relief was knowing she wasn't crazy. I think back to all the times I had thought she was out to lunch and regretted my choice of words when talking to her. I was happy for Seri and the progress she was making. I really was. She deserved to be happy. Lord knows, it was a long time coming. Selfishly, the more she regained control of her life, the more I hoped mine would improve too but so far, nada.

For Mom, therapy had made her feel more guilty. Of what, I couldn't be sure but my hunch was, she felt it was her fault Seri had been so low and believed life wasn't worth living. She shouldered all the blame and was going to spend the rest of her life making it up to Seri. In doing so, however, Mom was not living her life. She had forgotten how to smile. She didn't go anywhere in fear of what may happen while she was gone. The biggest thing she had forgotten was, she had a husband and not one but two daughters. That I needed love as much as Seri. But I couldn't tell her that. Not when we had almost lost Seri. Not when the image of her lying on the cold vinyl floor, life oozing out of her was still fresh in our minds. I wasn't that selfish... for the most part. However, anger was entering into my every-day emotions, and I didn't like it one bit. That's not who I was.

For a long time, Dad was the one who had understood how I felt and would pick up Mom's slack. He would take me for ice cream if Seri was sad and Mom had her snuggled up watching her favorite movie on the couch. If Seri got a bad grade in school, Mom soothed her by taking her for some "one on one" retail therapy. Dad would pipe up and say, "Hey, Ives, let's go play catch" to offset the fact I was once again left to my own devices. Dad was the reason I knew I was loved in our family. He always told me that Mom loved me. She was just worried about Seri. Even if Mom's actions didn't mirror Dad's words, I knew he would never lie to me. If he said Mom loved me, well then, maybe she did.

But so much had changed that terrible night. Dad was no longer sure of his place in our family, and he had no hope to offer me. He was never home anymore and when he was, he had no patience for anyone or anything. He never went to see Mom in the shop or ask her about her day. He stopped asking me to play catch or throw a Frisbee around. That used to be our thing. We would head out into the yard and find something to do and chat about life. Dad used to think I was a hoot, but he doesn't hear a word I say anymore. He was happier leaving the house than he was coming home. He didn't know what to say to any of us. I wasn't sure what to say to him either to help restore our bond. "Hey, Dad, you hate Mom too?" didn't seem like appropriate talk. Neither did, "I think my sister has had enough of Mom's attention for a lifetime, don't ya think?"

Staying quiet was definitely the best option considering the frame of mind I was in lately. It wasn't Dad I was angry with. I shoved the blame onto Mom for ignoring Dad. I knew exactly how he felt. He was missing her like I had been for a long time. To be honest, she was the best part of our family. She had a fun personality and the loudest laugh. While she was cringe-worthy when she made an outburst at the rink and had embarrassed me many times, her enthusiasm always made me smile. The kindness in her heart was second to none, and she cared for everyone she came across, including members of the opposing team. But now, she couldn't let go of her obsession with Seri. She was lost in guilt, grief and sadness. As much as it made me sad to see my mother a totally different person, it angered me more than anything.

But I said nothing of all these distressing changes to our family make-up and watched her continue to cater to Seri. Mom had even made Seri and I switch rooms when Seri had returned home from the hospital so Seri was directly across the hall from her and Dad. At the time, I was told it was a temporary move.

"You can have your room back in a few months, Ivy. This is so I can keep a closer eye on Seri. We need to make sure she is okay. I need to hear her if she gets up in the night."

It wasn't a total hardship to give up the room, but it made me feel less important. Like my life and my problems weren't as worthy. I had asked for a window seat in my room when the house had been built. I loved nothing more than to curl up with a good book in the cozy space, the sunlight pouring onto the pages and being transported into whatever magical fairy tale world I was reading about. I would look out over the vast garden Mom had grown and imagine the characters of my book hidden throughout it, each row a different land. Seri hadn't wanted a window seat, so now I had to plunk down on her springy mattress when I had the desire to read, and I had no view of the backyard. It didn't give my books the same reading appeal. I glanced at the book I had started four months ago, with the spine still intact, no further than page seven. I would have devoured that book in my old room.

Petty, was how I felt when I thought that, and I replayed what Mom had voiced when I had brought it up a few weeks ago...

"Hey, Mom, do you think I could switch rooms with Seri? I miss reading at the window seat."

"I didn't know you couldn't read anywhere else other than on that seat. Is it really so important? We had agreed that your sister needed your room until we knew she was okay."

"Well, it's been four months, is all. I just thought that maybe it was time. Seri seems better than ever." My hope had slipped away, and shame rose in my cheeks for asking.

Mom had spun around and sharply replied, "Well, I didn't know there was a timeline on healing, and that reading had to be done in a certain spot. If that's your biggest worry of the day, I envy you. When I am ready for her to go to the end of the hall, you'll be the first to know."

The conversation was brief but hurtful all the same. I felt conflicting emotions. Shame for suggesting the change after my sister's fateful night and post diagnosis, but a larger part of me felt shunned and angry. Didn't Mom know I needed to feel like I mattered too?

Weeks turned into months, time vanishing as quickly as the morning dew on a sunny spring day. During this time, my emotions changed from sympathy for my sister's needs to jealousy because Mom didn't think I existed. It expanded to feelings of neglect and finally to brewing rage in the base of my stomach I didn't like nor cared for.

Anger reared its ugly head once more this morning when Mom passed my door. For the first time I could remember, I didn't feel like easing her or Seri's burden and pretend it didn't bother me that she treated us differently. That my sister took all of Mom's time and love. It changed Dad too, so much so, he didn't want to be around any of us. It bothered me. Very deeply, and I was tired of being an afterthought. I was tired of Mom walking by my door every morning without so much as a thought about me.

It wasn't a school day, so I didn't have to get up early, but my mood would bring no more sleep. I decided today was going to be the day I told Mom how I was feeling. Seri wasn't the only one learning from therapy. In our family session, we were told that communication was the only way our family would endure the hardships we faced, and it was time I was honest. Ready or not, Mom, here I come.

Gathering the first clean clothes I found on my floor, I hopped into the hot shower, trying to wash away the hurt and rage that had been building inside for years. I wanted to be in a good frame of mind to talk to Mom.

The water beat down on my skin, and its warmth relaxed me. Until a knock on the bathroom door made me bristle. I knew who it was before she spoke.

"Hey, Ivy... you almost done?" Just as I had thought. It was Seri's voice wafting through the door.

"No, I'm not. I just got in." Short and to the point. I felt anger bubbling again.

"Well, I need in too. Can you hurry?"

"I could, but we have two bathrooms, so use the other one!"

"I don't want to go downstairs. Hurry up!"

I was growing angrier by the second. I had planned on taking a short shower, but my plans changed. I would stay in here until suppertime.

Seri continued to bang on the door, doing what she could to piss me off when Dad came to the door and sided with her.

I didn't bother to reply to him. I was too mad and hurt. Steam rose from both me and the shower head. It was never going to end. They were never going to understand what it was like to live and not be seen.

"Did you hear me, Ivy? I said, hurry up!"

"I heard. I'll hurry for the princess," was my sarcastic reply. "It's not a school day, you know. She doesn't need to get anywhere!" I tossed out this piece of information to try and win him over, but to no avail.

"I don't care what day it is. Get your ass moving. You aren't the only one who needs the bathroom."

I felt like crying. It hadn't always been like this between Seri and me. We had our moments, sure, but for the most part, we used to be best friends. Growing up, we had the same set of friends and did everything together. Seri had stuck pretty close to me my whole life and although I knew why now, it was still a tight bond for the most part.

I had seen the struggles she dealt with but really didn't understand the extent of them until recently. Until I had almost lost her. Her pain was real. She had her demons but sweet blue cricket shit, I had feelings too!

I tried to defuse my anger by thinking of all Seri had been through in her lifetime. The first thing I had picked up on when we were little girls was how she had to repeat most things she would say. At night, for example, she always said, "Night. Love you. Stay close at all times." She would have to say it three times and by the third time, our father would lose his patience. If we tried to cut her off before she finished, she would tear up and eventually sneak out of bed to get the last two times said out loud. She knew Dad was going to get angry when she got out of bed, but it was like she couldn't help herself. One time, she even got a spanking, but that was more acceptable to her than not being able to repeat the phrase three times.

That memory made me think of recess in elementary school when Seri had gotten a detention. The lunch lady had warned her several times to stop asking the same questions. The lady would yell to all of us to line up, and Seri would run up to her and say, "We going in now? You want us in the line, right?" The answer was always yes, but Seri would rephrase the question again. "So, right now we are going in, and we need to stand here. Correct?"

Every single day, it was the same questions. The lunch lady had finally had enough and told Seri that if she asked again, she could stay inside the following day. I figured the lady thought Seri was mocking her. But really, it was a habit Seri's mind couldn't break. Sure enough, the question was asked three times despite the warning, and I was having recess outside alone the following day.

I sighed and rinsed the shampoo out of my hair. My anger softened, and pity slowly took over. I couldn't relate to Seraphina sometimes, but it hadn't been easy for her. It had to be suffocating to be trapped and not be able to get out of her own head. I saw Seri battle many panic attacks in her day to know the struggle was real. She told me after she started therapy that it was like her mind would not listen to what she was telling it. It was its own entity and couldn't care less what Seri wanted. But she was healing now, and Mom needed to understand that.

Stepping onto the beige, plush bath mat Mom had recently bought, I dried off, brushed my teeth and surveyed myself in the mirror, looking away just as quickly. I was usually happy with the image I saw, but the girl who stared at me today was older and pretty grumpy looking. I reminded me of my mother. Scary thought.

I dressed as slowly as I could without running the risk of Dad yelling again but long enough to provoke Seri to pound on the door to get in. I opened the door and pushed past her, making sure she felt some of my body on the way by. In hockey, we called that rubbing them out on the boards.

"Feel better about yourself, Ivy?" Seri pushed back but only managed to bounce off me. A happy result of being the much taller sibling. She didn't stand a chance in any physical altercation.

"You know what? I really do, you impatient, needy ass hat. Hope you don't need hot water." Satisfied I had made her feel as miserable as I did, I skipped breakfast and headed out to the garden, where Mom would be. I hoped that perhaps today, she would take me driving, since she had nothing on the go. I hadn't been out very often since I had gotten my fulls last week. I wasn't comfortable driving alone yet, even though I could.

"Morning, Mom." I sat on the bench beside where she was pulling out weeds from around the sunflowers. "Getting lots done?"

She turned and smiled. "I am actually. Although it's getting hot quickly. Won't be out long today, I don't think."

I was encouraged by this news. "So, what about you and I taking a drive into town today then? Do some shopping or go for lunch somewhere. I can practice driving. We haven't had any you and me time in awhile."

Mom's answer was quick, without giving much thought to my feelings.

"I would love to! I had the same thoughts myself. Let me check with Seri first. I don't think she has plans, so she may want to come."

Had Mom even heard what I had asked? I asked for her. Not me, her and Seri.

"Not that I don't want Seri to come or anything. It's just I thought you and I could have some you and me time. I haven't had much of your attention since... Well, you know..." I did all I could not to sound like I was making this all about me. I clenched my hands together, willing her to understand.

Mom stood and was almost eye to eye with me, even though I was sitting on the pallet bench.

"She may not even want to go. Run and check with her, and see what she'd like to do. If she is fine staying home, well, we can scoot out quickly for an ice cream or something." Like a bug, I was swatted away. "If she decides to come, maybe we could make a day of it."

"Never mind. We'll do it another time."

"What? No, today is a great day. We haven't had a girls' day in ages. With the three of us." She was determined to keep Seri in our plans.

"Mom, usually it's you and Seri together. I don't say much to you about it, but I would really like you and I to have a day together, even just a few hours. Seri will be fine without you."

She turned and studied my face. I don't know what she was looking for. Maybe she was trying to read my thoughts.

"I highly doubt she will want to come anyways, but it's not a chance I want to take. If she doesn't want to come, that's fine, but we at least ask her to come, or we don't go."

"Then I guess we don't go. I'll go myself."

The hurt in my voice was lost on her because she steered the wheelbarrow to the compost bin and said over her shoulder, "Suit yourself, Ivy."

At that moment, I wanted to cry. I wanted to yank out every single plant Mom had lovingly cared for. I wanted her to feel the despair I was feeling. Instead, I turned around and stomped into the house to grab my wallet. I'd go myself. I wasn't staying here to watch Mom entertain Seri. Storming up the stairs brought no response from Mom. Tears of desperation threatened to spill over. I slid the patio door so hard, it almost flew off the track.

"Hey, Ivy, want to..." Seri, sensing my mood, didn't finish that sentence and instead asked, "What crawled up your ass?" She was sitting at the kitchen table eating a bowl of cereal, oblivious, as usual, to the tension she was responsible for.

"Would it really matter what I am feeling, Seri? Shouldn't we all ask you how you are today? After all, you are the special child. The important child. Hell, basically their only child."

Not waiting for a reply, I marched past the table and down the hall to my room. I slammed the door shut and locked it. The tears that had threatened a few minutes earlier came spilling down my cheeks. They fell fast and furious like hot lava spewing out of an active volcano. My pent-up rage bubbled over, and I felt like smashing something. I felt reckless, lonely and unwanted. Years of hurt churned in my heart and when pacing the room was not relieving my frustration, I shoved my wallet into my pocket, raced outside and hopped into the car.

Screw them. I'd enjoy the morning alone. Maybe head to the beach. I wasn't big on swimming, but I sure did love a beach walk along the water's edge. Blinding rage had full control over me. It frightened me but also powered my determination. I found the key in the middle console and rammed it into the ignition.

I started the car and revved the engine for no particular reason other than I was angry, and I knew this would piss off Mom if she heard it. Throwing it into reverse, I backed up, narrowly missing the ditch on the left side of the driveway. Thrusting the car into gear, I stopped for a split second to look back at my home, what was supposed to be my happy place. I paused, willing someone, anyone in my family to notice I was leaving. For Mom to come running over to tell me to wait, she would come after all. Stop me... Love me, I silently pleaded, but no one appeared.

I threw the car into drive and squealed my tires to the best of my ability on the gravel road. I would enjoy the day despite my family. I didn't need them either. Not realizing I picked up speed at an alarming rate the farther down the road I travelled, I had no idea just how sorry Mom was going to be that she had decided to brush me off.

Seraphina

The door quietly shut behind Mom after she came in to check on me. I heaved a sigh of relief that she thought I was sleeping. I knew this was her morning routine, and no one was going to stop it. I found an odd comfort in her being so close, right across the hall and yet at the same time, I felt stifled. I had no one to blame for her constant state of worry, but I wished she would get as much out of therapy as I was getting.

That first night in the hospital, after I had made the worst decision of my life, was a blur. I had no real recollection of what was going on. I vaguely remembered Mom stroking my hair, and Dad telling me he loved me. A distant voice told them I needed a blood transfusion, and then it went blank until the following afternoon. It scared me at first, when I woke up and Mom and Dad weren't with me. I was convinced they had given up on me. When I was informed they had been sent home so doctors could evaluate me, I felt relief they hadn't shunned me for the terrible stunt I had pulled.

The staff I had met at the hospital were very understanding. There was no judgement, only genuine interest to get to the bottom of my issues and make sure there was never a repeat of what had transpired. Maybe it was lack of sleep, lack of blood or just lack of caring that I opened up fully and whole-heartedly to the therapist I had been introduced to when I was coherent enough to speak. I was asked what drove me to do what I had done. The Voice was subdued, like it understood I had survived its worst attack, and that I could survive whatever it wanted to throw at me now.

For the first time in my life, I felt understood. I felt sane. It felt like I could be whole. A name was given to my battles, and I was thrilled to realize I wasn't alone. OCD and anxiety were more common than I had known, and many people struggled with their own thoughts. Well, thrilled wasn't the right word because it broke my heart that others struggled with this too, but to know I wasn't crazy was healing. Mom saw the difference in me right away. When she came to the hospital a few days later, she told me I looked like the weight of the world had come off my shoulders, and she wasn't wrong. We laughed, hugged and talked about everything and anything. She didn't claim to understand what I had been through, but I saw the immense relief my healing was bringing her. But as therapy continued and I reclaimed more of my mind, Mom and Dad struggled and grew apart. I think they had trouble getting past the guilt they carried. I couldn't imagine what it was like for them as parents to see their child this way, but it was not something they would easily forget. None of us would ever be able to block that night out, but I wanted us to move forward as a family.

I ran a finger over the scar on my left wrist. The surgeon had done a wonderful job sewing up the wounds, and I could barely feel a height difference between my scar and wrist. The scar was turning white, and in some spots was barely visible. As strange as it sounded, I didn't want it to fade completely. I hated that I had done this, but it was a constant reminder that it was okay to ask for help because if I didn't, this was the alternative. I would struggle with OCD and The Voice for the rest of my life, but it was manageable if I took the help from my therapist and from those who loved me the most. So, if I had to endure Mom's morning check-ins, well, that was a small price to pay for what I had put her through.

I sat up in bed and repositioned the pillows to support my back. I heard Mom in the kitchen, and I wanted to wait until she went out to the garden before I got up. Not that I was avoiding her exactly. I just had a hard time watching her struggle between being overprotective and nonchalant. She couldn't figure out how much space to give me, and it was painful watching her struggle with how to talk to me. Maybe I was learning avoidance from my father. He was as rare a sighting lately as a shooting star. When I did see him, he was sad and often distant with little to say. When not at work, he was holed up in the rec room or in his bedroom, sleeping. I wasn't even sure if he and Mom spoke to each other anymore.

They were like ships passing in the night and what was worse, I think they were beginning to be okay with that. I wondered if we were going to figure out how to be a family again. While I didn't miss my old self, I missed how much my parents loved each other and loved Ivy and me. I missed their stolen kisses when they thought no one was watching, the laughter Ivy brought to our lives, and the love that radiated through the house when Mom cranked the tunes and made us laugh with her foolishness. I couldn't remember the last home-cooked meal we sat down to and enjoyed. It was so ironic that as I tightened the reins on the beast in my mind that everything else spiralled out of control.

I stiffened when I heard someone in the hall. It must have been Ivy. She was not a morning person, so I assumed she was up to use the bathroom, and then she'd return to bed. Some things with me hadn't changed. I still took my morning shower at 8:00 am, and it was only three minutes away from that deadline.

Throwing off the sheet that was on top of me, I picked out an outfit for the day. I had no real plans, but I was thinking I might visit a friend who had stopped in to see me when I was at my lowest. I had known Christian since kindergarten. He had always tried to talk to me and was so sweet in trying to include me whenever something was going on at school. We didn't hang out often growing up because I was embarrassed to be around people due to the inner battle with the idiot in my brain. Now that I saw things clearly, I was learning to branch out and trust those who wanted to be my friend. I was really surprised when Christian came to the house the third week I was home and ask me what I was struggling with. All he knew was, I wasn't in school, and he was concerned. I thought about lying to him. Telling him I had a virus or chicken pox or anything that would have me out of school for a few weeks but one thing I had been taught early in therapy was, mental illness was not something to be embarrassed about. It was the fourth leading cause of death around the world, and on its way to surpassing heart disease. That was a scary fact. So, I took a deep breath and explained to Christian what had happened. His reaction was not what I had expected. I was waiting for his disbelief or him thinking I had done this for attention. I was waiting for him to laugh or call me dramatic. He did none of that. Instead, I saw genuine concern and the glistening of tears in his eyes as I quietly told him of all I had been through. He was nothing but supportive, and he was exactly what I never knew I needed. My family had to love me; it was just the way of it. But Christian could have walked away any time during my story, and yet he stayed. He listened and believed me. He saw the bad and ugly of who I was and still wanted to be my friend.

We got closer every day, and I had a true best friend in him. He became as close to me as Mari was. Mari had checked in with me every day since that night, and we never parted ways without her saying she loved me. It was another marvellous part of my healing. Learning to trust others and learning that if someone doesn't like me, that's on them, not me. I am enough. And I am worthy.

I opened the door and stepped into the hall. Ivy was still occupying the bathroom. Well, wasn't that a real treat? She knew this was the time I showered every single day. And yet, here she was, soaking up the hot water with no plans to go anywhere. I was sure of it. I decided to wait a few minutes, hoping she was at the tail end of her shower. Lots had changed for me in a short time, but I still had daily rituals I couldn't break. This was one of them. One battle at a time.

Ivy was very sensitive lately. The first few months after that night, she had been overly kind to me, even giving up her room so Mom could have peace of mind with me next to her, but that didn't last long. Ivy was increasingly bitter with me. Or maybe it was Mom she had the beef with. It was hard to say. Not until I was forced to look at my life did I realize how left out Ivy must have felt all those years. Mom always fussed over me. It was always me they comforted when something went wrong. Everything was about me. It must have been a huge disappointment to Ivy now that I was doing better that things for her were worse. Mom went from worrying I might do something drastic to fearing I'd do something worse than what I'd done. No matter how many times I tried to reassure her, she wouldn't let it sink in that I was going to be okay. And I was. I knew I may fall here and there, but I was never going down that dark, lonely, frightful road again. I knew what I was battling, and I was a warrior. I would fight tooth and nail to stay with my family. Therapy would be a part of my life forever because I never wanted to feel that low again.

"You don't know that for sure, Seri. I still live in your mind."

The Voice sounded pouty this morning, like a kid not allowed to eat candy before supper. "I know exactly where you are, and I am no longer afraid of you," came my silent reply. The Voice was more persistent today than it had been in weeks.

"You don't have to be afraid. We can be friends, you know."

"No, thanks. You're not worthy of my time." Although I won the conversation like I had been doing for months now, it still put me on edge that I still heard The Voice from time to time. Slightly agitated, I decided I had waited long enough for Ivy to get out of the shower. "Hey, Ivy, you almost done?" I asked as nicely as I could muster.

"No, I'm not. I just got in," came the reply. Which was a lie. She had been in there for at least 15 minutes. What was she doing, and what was with the shitty attitude she was giving me?

"Well, I need in too. Can you hurry?"

"I could," she yelled back, "but we have two bathrooms, so use the other one!"

Ugh, now I was getting mad. Obviously if I wanted to go downstairs, that's where I would be. I used this shower this time of day, every day. Why would I risk having to listen to the damn voice in my head if I changed my routine? As I said, some things had drastically changed for me, while others were still a work in progress, and my morning ritual was not something I had mastered yet. It needed to stay the same for now.

"I don't want to go downstairs. Hurry up!" I yelled and incessantly pounded my fist on the door to bring home my point. On what could have been the hundredth bang, I glanced over my shoulder to see Dad storming down the hall toward me, not looking pleased. Instead of yelling at me, he spoke through the bathroom door.

"Ivy, just hurry up, okay? Your sister doesn't shower downstairs, and you know it. Why do we go through this every day?"

Dad spun around and looked me square in the eye. Speaking softly and precisely, he said, "Seri, I know you have been doing great with your progress, but little things like this need to stop, okay? Start working on changing your daily routine. I think you can handle showering downstairs or finding the patience to wait until Ivy is done. This is the last time I am coming to your defence on this issue." He turned to the door and since we still heard water coming out of the shower head, he yelled again. "Did you hear me, Ivy? I said, hurry up!"

"I heard. I'll hurry for the princess," came Ivy's sarcastic reply. "It's not a school day, you know. She doesn't need to go anywhere!"

"I don't care what day it is. Get your ass moving. You aren't the only one who needs the bathroom."

With that, Dad looked at me one more time as if to say, wait your turn, and walked out of the house. Another fine start to the day in the Bartley household. I considered returning to my room to wait but thought better of it. Ivy should be out any minute. She hated when Dad yelled, and it only took once for him to get her to do what he wanted her to. Years ago, she had told me his loud voice went right through her and sent shivers up her spine.

I guess that effect was over because according to my watch, another nine minutes had passed, and still no Ivy. The water hadn't been running for a bit, so I assumed she was dressing blindfolded and making her own toothpaste. I pounded on the door again. This kid was really pushing my buttons today.

Ivy appeared and bumped into me on her way by. I tried to push back but let's be real; she towered over me and liked me knowing it. I could only use words to fight back.

"Feel better about yourself, Ivy?"

She smiled a devilish little smile and replied, "You know what? I really do, you impatient ass hat. Hope you don't need hot water."

She was hoping to piss me off and frankly, it had worked. I slammed the bathroom door shut, and it vibrated on its hinges. No hot water. Great. I grabbed the toothbrush while I waited for the hot water tank to rejuvenate. This was enough of a change in my routine that The Voice wanted to be heard.

"This isn't how we do things, Seri. Shower first, and then—"

"I don't give two shits about what you want! I'm brushing my teeth!"

It felt so good to be strong enough to silence The Voice, but I felt serious apprehension about the order in which I was doing things. However, I was not going to be swayed. I slopped the toothpaste onto the brush and began fighting plaque. And guess what? The world didn't end like The Voice thought it would. Like The Voice had conditioned me to believe. Another small victory, and I loved it! My mood was definitely shifting back to happy. Maybe after I showered, I would ask Ivy if she would like to come with me to Christian's, and then maybe head to the beach to combat the heat that was already on the rise.

I was pleasantly surprised at the temperature coming out of the shower head. I didn't like the water too hot on days like this anyway. I found if I let the water go cold the last minute or so, when I stepped out into the heat, it was more welcoming than stifling. Once I was done in the bathroom, I went to the kitchen.

It was still hard to enter the kitchen, but I pushed through my negative thoughts and hummed a song I had heard on the radio the other day. If I concentrated on the lyrics, there was no room for The Voice. A wonderful and effective therapy technique. I grabbed a bowl of Shreddies and blueberries (what I liked to think of as breakfast of champions) and sat down at the island Dad had built while I was in the hospital recovering. As I scooped up another delicious bite, I heard Ivy clunking up the stairs, then the patio door slammed open.

"Hey, Ivy, want to..." I didn't finish my question. It was clear she was in a foul mood. Fighting with Mom again, no doubt. She had a hate on for Mom, but, geez, it wasn't easy for her. "What crawled up your ass?"

"Would it really matter what I am feeling, Seri? Shouldn't we all ask how you are today? After all, you are the special child. The important child. Hell, basically their only child." With that, she stormed to her room.

I sat there for a minute, digesting not only my cereal, but what Ivy had said. It was clear she had meant every word, and it dawned on me that I had been right. Ivy did feel left out. She did feel that none of us cared for her. That couldn't have been further from the truth. Ivy was one of the reasons I got up and fought my demons every day. She was the only one who didn't wear kid gloves around me. She was my sister, and I loved her very much. I wasn't sure if I should go to her or talk to Mom. It was time Mom understood how deep Ivy's hurt feelings went. I had a sneaking suspicion she was oblivious to this fact.

The decision was made for me when I heard Ivy throw open her door, heard it crash into the wall, and then saw her fly down the stairs. I wanted to go after her, but I thought better of it. I would wait until the anger passed. Too many times things were said in anger we couldn't take back, and our family wasn't in a place we could rebound from cruelty. When I heard Ivy revving the car, I changed my mind. She shouldn't be driving when she was that mad. I quickly took my bowl to the sink and ran to the closet to find sandals to slip on. By the time I got out the door, she was gone. Guess it was time to have a conversation with Mom instead.

I walked around the side of the house and found Mom at the compost pile, shovelling the grossest-looking stuff from one pile to another. Turning it, was what she called it. I described it as disgusting.

"Mom, Ivy just left here, and she was pretty upset." I started the hard conversation. "Do you know what was bugging her?"

She stopped shovelling, wiped sweat from her eyes and leaned on the shovel. "Honestly, no. She asked me if we could spend the day together, and I thought it was a great idea. I asked her to go see what you wanted to do, and that's when she got pissy."

There it was. Why Ivy was mad. "Ivy wanted to spend time with just you. Without me. She never gets your time without me around." I watched to see if this was registering with her. I didn't want to hurt her, but she needed to see Ivy and her pain too. I wasn't the only one suffering. She started shovelling again, and then paused.

"What difference would it make if we all went?" She was rationalizing her fears and struggling with the reality in front of her. She was now losing Ivy, instead of me.

"Mom, I'm so sorry for what I did." Without warning, tears fell quickly and freely. "I know you wake up every day and in your mind, see me on the floor dying. I can never make that up to you. But what I can tell you is, I have never felt more in control of myself as I do now."

I stepped closer to bridge the gap between us. "I don't blame you for a single thing. Not one. You had no idea what I was dealing with. I didn't tell you. And that's on me." I paused for a moment to regain some composure. "But what is happening now is, you're forgetting to love Ivy. You don't pay any attention to Dad. All you do is worry about me. It has consumed you. And it's stifling for all of us."

I hadn't been looking directly at her when I was talking, but I ventured a look now. She was crying too. She was making no attempt to hide that from me. This was new.

"Mom, say something. I don't mean to hurt you. I just can't watch my family fall apart anymore because of me."

She slowly walked to the bench nestled amongst the garden. I wasn't sure if she was going to speak. I wasn't sure if she could with how hard she was crying.

"I – I don't know what to say. It's never been your fault. None of this is. I blame myself. How can a mother not know her own child is suffering?" A strangled noise from the depths of her soul escaped with the word suffering. She was shattering like the clay pot I had found in the garden shop the day after I had overheard her and Dad arguing. Hurt spilled through every pore like the jagged shards had spattered across the floor.

"I see you're getting better. I'm overjoyed. I am." She gulped for air. "But I feel lost. I don't know what to do. How can I let go? I could see your pain, but I couldn't see how deep it ran within you. I'm afraid I won't see it again. How can I trust you will be okay?" She drew a ragged breath. "I haven't been giving anyone attention. I know that." She stood and paced between the bench and me and attempted to dry her eyes with the back of her hands. "I know in my heart, I pushed Ivy to the side. I have been distant with your father. But I was scared. I still am scared that if I turn my back on you, for even a second, I will lose you." A sob wracked her, and she bent over, both hands on her knees.

I went to her and rubbed her back gently. "Just breathe, Mom. There you go." Her heart rate slowed, and she began to concentrate on her breathing.

"You won't lose me now, Momma. I promise. And if I do get low again, which we know is a real possibility, I will never ever keep you in the dark. Okay?" I hoped my words were soothing. I meant every one. I hated to see her like this. The dam had broken, and she was a sight I had never seen before.

"I look at the scars on my wrists when I get up every morning and when I go to bed each night. They are a constant reminder of how close I came to losing my family. I never ever want to go back there either. You guys mean too much to me."

She considered what I'd said. "I love you all the same, you know." She reached for me and held me tightly. "I never loved you more than Ivy. You needed me more. At least, I thought you did. I thought I was going to lose you. And I wasn't wrong. I did almost lose you." She sighed into my hair.

"I know that. But I am not so sure Ivy gets it. She wants to, but she needs you. She loves you so much. And Dad loves you too. He misses you." My therapist was as sharp as a tack and had helped me see how my struggles had affected my family.

"When did you get so wise?" Mom took me by the shoulders and held me out in front of her to get a better look.

"I'd like to say I was always a smartie, but Denise deserves the credit." It did my heart good to hear her laugh.

"I'll have to thank her then." She took me by the hand, and we walked towards the house. "Maybe I should start listening to her in my sessions." We were almost to the house when she added, "I think I'll call Ivy and spend the day with her after all." She looked at me to see if I was okay with this, which I certainly was. "No time like the present to make amends, right? Think I can convince her to come back for me?" No sooner had she spoken those words, and the cell phone in her apron pocket rang.

"Maybe that's her," I said optimistically.

"Maybe." She put her phone on speaker. "Hello?" As we listened to the person on the other end of the call, we knew there would be no making amends with Ivy today.

Dexter

The sun must have been up. More reliable than the sun itself, my wife was sitting on the edge of our queen-size bed, no doubt her mind racing and worrying about the only thing she was capable of thinking about anymore: Seri.

I wasn't sure I was ready to get up and face another day of the scorching heat we were being pummelled with this year, but one thing was for certain; I was not in the mood to deal with Adalynn. I was tired of being the last thing on her mind and listening to her constant worry over our daughter. I was tired of rehashing the past.

What we did wrong, what we could have done differently, what we missed and on and on the list went. I still harboured resentment towards Adalynn. I thought she sheltered Seri too much, hovering over her constantly, even when she was little. Damn it, lately I blamed Addie for my own mental state. She was driving me completely mad with her aloofness towards me. Not that she didn't have grounds to be mad with all the bad words between us, but it was time to move forward. It wasn't healthy for any of us to live like this.

Or maybe I didn't want to talk about what happened because I denied anything was ever wrong in the first place. Addie had sensed something in Seri when she was little that I hadn't picked up on. Part of me was pissed off I hadn't seen what was in front of me. I knew everything wasn't all right, yet when Addie pointed out the issues, I kept telling her it was fine, to leave Seri be. Her routine of repeating herself should have revealed the problem, but I ignored it and at times, it frustrated me, especially her nighttime routine.

"Night, Mommy and Daddy. I love you... I love you guys so much. Good night." And then finally, "Night, night. Sleep tight. Love you guys."

Every single night. It never changed. But I had brushed off Adalynn time and time again, telling her it was just a silly habit Seri had. We all had our weird quirks.

The truth of the matter was it wasn't only Addie I was angry with.

Maybe it was my own shortcomings that had me pretending to be asleep this morning to avoid her. Perhaps some part of her saw what I didn't want to admit: the blame rested on my shoulders. That I was Seri's dad, and she had always been daddy's little girl. We had been inseparable since she had taken her first steps. I didn't know how I could have been so blind to the battle that had ensnared Seri's thoughts on such a serious level for so long.

A bead of sweat formed on my brow. I couldn't decipher if it was from the rising heat or where my thoughts were headed. Thinking of what my family had been through was not something I could handle this morning, or any other time, so I did the only thing I could to avoid a fight with my wife. I pretended to be asleep while she got ready for her day.

However, I was still a man who longed for my wife. When I heard her feet touch down on the floor, creaking ever so slightly under her weight, I opened my eyes a bit and saw her reflection in the dresser mirror.

She still made my blood rush. As she pulled the black negligee over her head, I was flooded with the impulse to call her back to bed. Unknowingly seductive, she stood with her back to me, naked in all her splendour. Bending over to grab her shorts, I concentrated on not moaning out load. It had been months since I had touched her.

She was in good shape, even more so in the summer with the gardening she did. Her ass had reaped the rewards of countless hours spent hoeing, raking and tending to her pride and joy. I didn't much care for the vegetables she was growing, but I enjoyed the definition of her body each summer. My excitement grew as I watched her dress. She turned slightly, looking for a T-shirt and when she did, I saw her nipples had hardened, even in this heat. Her stomach was a sore spot for her, but the scars from the C-sections from our children only made me love her more. And I did. I loved my wife. I used to trace those scars at night, first with my finger and then with my lips, and tell her how much I appreciated the family she had given me. I almost called her to come back to bed where I could fulfill my desire for her. Almost.

What stopped me was doubt that she wanted me to touch her. She hadn't given any indication she cared if we were intimate or not. Her expression was forlorn while she quietly fastened her shorts, her fingers moving deliberately as if she was worried she'd wake me. Before our world changed, she would have given me a sly look and made sure I saw her changing. Teased me. Have me right where she wanted. The other night, she had come to bed and for a moment, I thought she had walked across our room to get my attention, bending over to look out the window, wearing a hot little nightie but as quickly as I thought it could have been for me, she hopped into bed and never so much as looked in my direction.

Adalynn had changed so much this last year. She was always lost in thought, slow to smile and never really in the present moment. She had a sense of humour that captivated a room (Ivy got her humour from her), but she hadn't so much as laughed in months. In the weeks following Seri's suicide attempt, I had been understanding and on edge myself. It was agonizing watching my kid suffer. Shattering to see someone I loved lying in a hospital fighting for her life, not only physically but mentally. If it had been physical ailments riddling Seri, I could have handled it. If I could see the problem and know what was needed, then this wouldn't have been such a challenge for me. I remembered when Seri had fallen off the bleachers when she was five years old. She had been chasing a foul ball, and her flip-flop got caught between the floorboards, propelling her forward and snapping her wrist in two places. I scooped her up into my arms, dried her tears and within a few hours, she had a cast on that traveled past her elbow.

That was the kind of pain I knew how to navigate. I had no clue how to help my daughter that night in the kitchen or any night since. I had no idea what mental anguish had led Seri down the path she was on. It left me feeling less of a man.

Therapy had been extensive for the entire family and while Seri was making giant steps in her recovery, Addie and I could not find our way back to one another. We kept drifting, and I had no idea how to pull her back to me.

As if to prove my point she was no longer interested in us, she walked into the hallway without so much as a backwards glance and entered Seri's room.

As quickly as the longing for my wife had come, it dissolved. I would wait until she was in the garden before I got up to go to work. Even though it was Saturday, I had taken on enough work to keep me away from home on weekends too. It was too draining to be here. Fifteen minutes or so passed before I felt it safe to get up and get dressed without running into Addie. Her worry still hung in the bedroom air, suffocating me, more so than the humidity. I couldn't wait to get out of the house if for nothing else but fresh air.

I walked to the door of our room and heard Seri and Ivy arguing. So much for a clean and quiet get-away. They were fighting over the bathroom. Why Seri had to stand outside the door the second her sister started the shower was a mystery that would never be solved. The girl needed her routine to flow with precision every single morning, or she didn't settle for the rest of the day. The number of routines she had to perform in the run of the day was shrinking, but the exact time she had to shower was not one of them. Again, something I simply couldn't relate to or comprehend. But Ivy should have known taking her sister's usual shower time would cause this uproar and frankly, it wasn't worth the crap that ensued.

I walked into the hallway, pushed Seri aside and banged on the bathroom door.

"Ivy, just hurry up, okay? Your sister doesn't shower downstairs, and you know that. Why do we go through this every day?" I waited a few seconds to calm down my tone and looked at Seri.

"I know you have been doing great with your progress, but little things like this need to stop, okay? Start working on changing your daily routine. I think you can handle showering downstairs or finding the patience to wait until Ivy is done. This is the last time I am coming to your defence on this issue." I returned my attention to the bathroom and repeated my demands to Ivy.

"I heard," came the reply from the other side of the door. "I'll hurry for the princess. It's not a school day, you know."

Her uncharacteristically sarcastic tone impressed me none, and I told her to get her ass moving. I gave Seri a look that said not to touch that door again until her sister came out and with that, I left the crumbling ruins that used to be my home.

Settling into my truck, I turned on the radio and cranked the tunes. Nothing like good music to forget my family troubles. I was genuinely looking forward to the renovation I was working on. Or, more accurately, who I was doing the reno for. I had met Sylvia a few months ago through another contractor who had been too busy to do the add-on to her home. She owned a little bungalow and wanted a sunroom in the rear, where she could enjoy her backyard view. What had struck me at our first meeting was Sylvia's amazing smile. It was genuine and touched her eyes, just like Adalynn's used to. Addie could light up a room with her playful nature, and her smile had made me take notice of her. Sylvia's smile brought back that memory so vividly, I instantly returned the smile. It had also renewed an easy-going feeling I hadn't felt in a long time.

After meeting with her a few times, I decided to do the reno, liking both the challenge of the job and the customer I was doing the project for. In the beginning, there were only conversations about the project. The flooring she wanted, the types of windows that could be installed, the pitch of the roof. She shared with me that this project was important to her because she needed a space to write at home, yet still have an impression she was somewhere else. As a freelance journalist, she had seen many parts of the world and wanted her backyard to feel like her personal oasis.

Her view of the river and the beautiful flower gardens she had landscaped over the last year was breathtaking, and I wanted this project to be just as magnificent for her.

A few weeks into the project, things changed. Subtle hints that maybe this could be more than a work relationship should either of us be interested in taking it further slipped into our body language and light conversation. I started working later hours and stayed behind to finish a few odds and ends that, in all honesty, could have been completed the following day with my crew.

A few nights, she cooked supper for me, and we sat on the lawn swing, taking in the sunset, listening to the rush of the river and talking for hours about nothing and everything. Sylvia had never married, had no kids. She wanted a career over family. She travelled all over the world and loved every minute of it. She had no regrets about her life choices and had no idea what it was like to have my kind of family issues. It was liberating to sit with her and not have to talk about anything other than our jobs and to live vicariously through her eyes as she told me about the world she had seen. I told her about my love for restoring old buildings and giving them new life and my passion for hockey, but I never talked about my family. That would have betrayed Addie. What was between Addie and I was ours, the good and the bad. Sylvia never asked. Whether it was because she didn't want to know, or she picked up on my reluctance to bring it up. Either way, we steered clear of family talk.

The first time Sylvia had leaned in and rested her head on my shoulder, we were slowly rocking back and forth on the swing enjoying a cold beer. I immediately thought back to mine and

Addie's first date. I still smelled her shampoo, a subtle nectarine scent. We had gone to a concert, and she was up dancing and singing along with the band. She leaned in at the end of the night, rested her head on my shoulder and whispered it was the best night of her life. She told me she had no doubt the best was yet to come. Sylvia's hair smelled different, more of a lavender scent, but the touch of a woman against me again felt nice.

I don't know why I didn't move Sylvia's head off my shoulder that first night or why the guilt that shot through me wasn't enough for me to get up and leave, but I stayed where I was and thought only of the moment I was in. Selfishly, I found comfort in this gesture. I felt desired again. I felt like a man with a purpose. That I was wanted by a woman. Not what I should have been thinking as a married man, but I was being honest to myself, and honesty sometimes hurts the ones we love the most. I told myself, it was why we weren't honest sometimes. It was why I had said nothing to Adalynn about any of this. I couldn't stand the thoughts of hurting her. We were both hurting enough as it was. But I felt a pull to this woman I was powerless to ignore.

Yanking my thoughts to the present, I pulled the truck into Sylvia's yard and was happy to see it was only her car in the driveway. No other contractors would be milling around today, so it would be just the two of us. Not sure if I was happier because I was working or because of the thoughts of seeing Sylvia, I grabbed my tool belt out of the back of the truck. As I came around the corner, there she stood, smiling and happy to see me. She was in a nightshirt that buttoned down to her knees, but she had neglected to fasten the first four buttons. I couldn't help but notice her breasts were firm and unrestrained.

"Morning, Dex. Nice of you to come today. I thought maybe you would take today off. It being Saturday and all." She walked towards me, turned at the patio doors and motioned for me to come into the kitchen.

"I couldn't think of anywhere I'd rather be today. I know how much you're looking forward to enjoying your sunroom."

I followed her inside and was surprised at the sadness I felt knowing the job was almost completed. That would mean no more excuses to see Sylvia.

Her kitchen was the biggest room in the home but the most warm and inviting. It was a country-styled kitchen with weathered cupboard doors and a maple countertop. It was equally tidy as it was cozy, and I smelled a warm drink brewing.

"Coffee?" Without waiting for an answer, she pulled two mugs out of the cupboard. As she reached up, the nightshirt went with her, exposing the length of her legs and the shape of her thighs.

"Sure." I couldn't think of anything to say. For once, I felt how Seri must have felt when her thoughts took over and she panicked, not knowing what side of her brain to listen to. In that instant, I fully understood the sheer magnitude of knowing how hard it was to make a decision that would impact not only me but everyone around me. To have a voice in my head telling me to be something I wasn't. Do something I never dreamed I was capable of. The inner struggle of good vs evil.

I was torn as to what side I was going to listen to.

At that moment, I wanted to bolt. To get back to my real life, not the life I presently existed in. I wanted the old life Addie and I had built together. The joy we used to share as a family. I wanted Addie so bad, it stung the back of my throat. To feel her touch me, to love her, to hold her and never let her go.

But also at that exact moment, my mind knew I couldn't get that back. That heading home would not give me any satisfaction, mentally or physically. That the woman before me was offering something Addie no longer wanted to give me. Her time. Her touch. She was willing to give herself to me, even if just for today.

As if sensing my hesitation, Sylvia set the mugs on the counter and walked towards me. She slowly closed the distance between us, hesitating slightly, giving me the time and space necessary to make my decision on what would happen next between us. We had been building up to this moment for a while now. I smelled her fragrance as she neared, a delicate vanilla scent. It was intoxicating.

I didn't allow myself to think of anything but this moment. I had become so good at shutting out my thoughts, it was scary how easy it was for me to take a step towards Sylvia. I reached out and put my hands on her hips and when she smiled in response, I thought of nothing but how her lips would taste. Her lips parted, and mine brushed hers ever so softly. Her arms circled my neck and pulled me down for a deeper kiss.

When the kiss deepened, so did my desire. My arms wrapped around her body and my hands rested on her buttocks. I pulled her as close to me as I could and when she moaned, I could no longer think of anything other than her.

Lust coursed through me, and I pinned her against the island so I got a better feel of her body. I ran my hand up under her nightshirt and cupped her perfectly-shaped breast. It felt warm and soft. I wondered for a brief moment if I was being too rough, but Sylvia was matching my intensity, undoing the buckle of my belt.

"Touch me," I whispered in her ear.

She undid my tool belt and tossed it to the floor. Her hands were fast, so quick I didn't realize she had undone my pants button until I felt her fingers encircle me. I groaned, incoherently. I was too far gone to give any thought to the guilt persistently ramming into my thoughts. Past thinking of what this would do to my family. What this would do to Addie. What it would do to my own conscience when this was over. I just wanted this moment and this moment only.

What made me stop what I was doing when my phone rang, I will never know. Was it guilt? Was it intuition knowing something was wrong?

"Damn," I groaned, breathlessly, and pulled the phone from my pocket. Adalynn.

"What?" Not the best way to answer, but it was all I had in me at that moment.

"Dex, it's Ivy. She's been in a car accident."

Adalynn

The ride to the hospital was like travelling back in time. The situations were completely different, but the sheer panic in my heart was identical. *This couldn't be happening again* was the only thought rattling around in my head, playing over and over like a broken record.

I looked at Dexter and could not decipher what he was thinking. His lips pressed firmly together was a good indication he was doing all he could to not speak and say something he may regret. He no doubt blamed me for Ivy's accident. It was the same facial expression he had worn before our previous fights. His knuckles were chalk white as he gripped the steering wheel. The speedometer told me his concentration was needed on the road, so I bit my lip and stayed silent. Guilt and grief washed over me as surely as waves had at the beach the last time I had been there. But there was no pleasure in this feeling. I reached into my purse sitting open on my lap, unsure how it had even gotten there, and searched for my puffer. The need to get my airways open was immense. Shake. Inhale. Hold breath. Breathe out. I repeated this twice, but no relief came.

"Put your head between your legs. You're starting to hyperventilate."

Dex's words sounded like they travelled through thick fog. I did as he said, and my breathing regulated itself, but nausea was on its heels.

How could this be happening? I should have been with her. How could Ivy have crashed the car so close to home? What had the police told me?

Ivy had crashed the car into a telephone pole and was at the hospital in critical condition. Oh, Ivy, why you? Was this somehow my fault too? My mind wouldn't stop. How had our family gotten to this point?

I didn't feel good about leaving Seri, but she was adamant about staying home and waiting for the news. I couldn't blame her. I didn't want to be making this drive. Or watch every agonizing minute tick slowly away on my watch, waiting for news. The thought of seeing Ivy's body broken and bruised terrified me, yet I was desperate to know how she was doing.

Strangely, I was relieved to realize not one ounce of my being was worried about Seri at this moment. The one and only good thing to come out of today.

Dex got us to the hospital in record time, but it still felt like I hadn't seen Ivy in years. I didn't wait for the truck to come to a full stop and jumped out, rolling my ankle in the process. Dex was saying something but at this point, I didn't care what he had to say. I wanted to get to Ivy. Limping across the parking lot, I entered the front revolving door. The hospital was surprisingly busy. Some people seemed fine and for a split second, it angered me that I was here for a much larger issue than a minor illness or injury.

Irrational thoughts aside, I focused on finding Ivy, but I was unsure of which way to go. A security guard, who must have picked up on my rising hysteria, approached calmly and asked if I was trying to get to a patient.

"Yes, I am. Ivy Bartley was brought in by ambulance... car accident. Please. I need to see her. She's my daughter." The words tumbled out. I was doing all I could not to lose the little control I had left.

"Come, sit. I will get an update and get you to her right away." She ushered me to the bench in the foyer and hurried to the reception desk to get the information.

Leaning over, I rested my head in my hands. I had to control my breathing. I wanted to be strong for Ivy. The one person in our family who didn't require my strength, who didn't demand my constant worry was suddenly in dire straits. I wanted to be there for her because she had always been there for anyone who had asked for help. She had always been the strong one. She had the biggest heart of anyone I've ever known. I couldn't let her down the one time she needed me.

A memory so vivid popped into my mind. Ivy was five years old, and I had tucked her in for the night. She had talked Dex and me into getting her a fish. A vibrantly-colored tropical fish she had named Felix the Fish Bartley.

Her eyes had been glued to the tank that night, taking in every inch of it. She ran her finger along the outside, following the path the fish was swimming, and her smile was as wide as the tank until she noticed the filter. It rested along the back of the tank with lots of little bubbles slowly levitating to the surface of the water.

"What's that mommy?"

"That's the tank's filter. It takes all the bad things in the water and gets rid of them."

She peered into the tank, and then said, "Can things get caught in there?"

"I don't think so. Anything that gets in the filter will get sucked up and taken away." Happy with my explanation for the five-year-old, I tucked her in snug as a bug in a rug and never thought about it again until she came flying into the living room a few minutes later, breathless but happy.

"Mommy, Mommy, come look! I saved Felix the Fish!!"

I ran down the hall with Ivy leading me by the hand and when I peered into the room, what I saw was ghastly. There, on the top of her bureau was Felix the Fish, her cute, innocent, colourful little fish, flapping around in desperate need of water.

"Ivy! Why did you do this?"

I quickly scooped up Felix and got him into the water. He didn't waste any time swimming and hiding behind the big rock at the bottom of the tank.

Crestfallen, Ivy, cried. "I saved him, Mommy. He was heading towards the filter, and I didn't want him to get sucked up, so I pulled him from danger! Why did you put him back in where the filter could get him?"

My heart burst with so much love as I relived the memory. That was Ivy in a nutshell. Always thinking of ways to save and love others, even if completely misguided.

A hand on my shoulder brought me back to the present moment. It was Dex.

"Where is she?" Pain was evident in his voice.

"I don't know yet. The security guard went to find out." As if on cue, the guard appeared and her facial expression told us how bad the situation was.

"Your daughter is in surgery. Go to the fifth floor. You can have a seat in the waiting room, where there is more privacy. You can speak with the doctors working on her when they are finished. They will find you there."

Working on her? I had heard that term before. That was not a good term for a parent to hear. That wasn't a good term for any loved one to hear.

I didn't think. I threw myself into Dex and began to weep. Violently the tears pushed past my resolve. I couldn't fight them any longer.

"Oh, Dex... not again... I can't do this again. Not with our Ivy."

I felt him shaking through my own vibrations. Our pain melded into one, and I felt the warm liquid of his tears accumulating in my hair. I couldn't remember Dex ever crying. Not even when Seri was in the hospital. It was going to be my undoing if I stood in his embrace any longer, so I pulled back, distancing myself from all the emotion. I didn't want to crumble when he needed me to be strong.

"Let's go. I'm ready." I wasn't ready, but I had no choice.

We shuffled to the elevator. I thought about taking the stairs as we stood waiting, but I didn't think my legs would work for that long. Just as well, the elevator doors opened a few seconds later, and we climbed on in silence. I stared at the buttons and realized all six of the passengers were going to the dreaded ICU. Every one of us was facing something we didn't want to see.

The elevator was noisy. Or maybe it was because I was holding my breath, I could hear everything that much more. The pulleys were straining to pull the weight of its cargo. Having no real knowledge of elevators, it seemed a good oiling was in order to get rid of the low-pitched squealing. If my thoughts had not been on such a traumatic situation, I may have asked out loud if elevators did in fact use oil. Dex always said I could question a person to death about the oddest and strangest things at the most random times.

The short ride was over, and I stepped out and into the intensive care unit. The feeling was all too familiar, and the ground seemed to sway beneath me like the haunted houses we used to visit at the fair.

Dex grabbed my elbow to help steady me. Or was it to steady himself? I held tightly to the railing that lined the hallway for extra support. The closer we got to the waiting room, the worse my balance became.

The waiting room was at the end of the hallway, and I was relieved to see there was no one occupying it. The other elevator passengers must have known where their loved ones were because no one followed us into the room. A faded black leather couch and a red beat-up La-Z-Boy took up most of the space. A tiny television was mounted in the corner of the room with a shelf situated underneath where the remote was. I sat down on the couch and began a prayer. The only thing I knew I could do in this situation.

Dex chose to stand and pace. A quick glance in his direction, and I saw the toll this was taking on him. I tried to find words to comfort him, but I couldn't bring myself to think of anything to say. The cold hard fact was, I felt like a stranger to him. I didn't know if he cared about how I felt. So instead of asking him to hold me like I desperately needed, I turned the conversation to the kids.

"Should we call Seri? Let her know we are here and will call her when we know something?"

He slowed his pace and looked at me. "I'm really not concerned about Seri right now."

His reply irked me. Did he not think I understood Ivy was our focus? I was in no mood to be criticized. "I realize she isn't top priority at this moment, but she's likely worried too. I'll call her myself." I stormed out of the waiting room and into the bathroom a few doors down.

Seri picked up on the second ring. "How is she, Mom? She okay?"

"Not sure yet, honey. She's in surgery. No one has come to see us yet. How are you?"

"Don't worry about me. I'm fine. I promise."

For some reason, I knew what she was saying was true. She would be fine. She had come a long way in a short time.

"Okay, we'll call you once we have an update. If you need me, just text or call, okay? Did you want to me to call Nanny to come stay with you while you wait?"

Seri liked the idea of company but said she would call her grandmother. We said our good-byes, and I headed back to the waiting room. Dex had finally taken a seat in the La-Z-Boy and had his eyes closed.

An hour passed and then two. Dex made no attempts to comfort me, nor I him. We were lost in our own worlds. When I thought I couldn't wait any longer, a man appeared in the doorway wearing operating scrubs with his surgical hat in his hand.

"Mr. and Mrs. Bartley?" he softly asked.

I didn't want to be Mrs. Bartley at that moment. I wanted to be anyone else. He seemed too solemn to be bringing good news. I didn't have to reply though because Dex did.

"Yes, that's us."

"Please have a seat."

I realized he was talking to me as Dex was already in the chair. This was not good. I sat down and braced myself for the verbal blows he was getting ready to launch at me.

"My name is Dr. Vanderbelt. I was the neurosurgeon on call when your daughter was brought in. Dr. Evette was the trauma surgeon on duty, and together we handled Ivy's surgery." His tone was matter of fact. Like he was reading a well-rehearsed script.

"Your daughter was in a significant accident today. There's no easy way to tell you what I have to say. While we stopped the internal bleeding, we had to remove her left kidney. The damage was too severe to save the organ." He sat down beside me on the couch and put his hand on mine. I remembered back to when Seri was in the hospital and drew from experience that it was harder for doctors than they were allowed to let on. His hand was cold, reminding me of the cold, sterile room Ivy lay in as they fought to save her life. Oddly, at that moment, I felt like comforting him.

"She also broke several bones, including her femur and wrist on her left side and her collar bone, but the injury I am most concerned with is her brain. When she was first brought in, she was conscious and able to talk but once surgery started, things started to get intense. She had cerebral edema. Simply put, her brain was swelling, and we had to drill a hole in her skull to help relieve the pressure."

I wasn't ready for his words. I could not process anything he said after the part of Ivy's brain swelling. He was still talking, and I thought Dex had asked a question, but I tuned out. I couldn't take any more bad news. I thought if I didn't hear it, it couldn't be true.

"Can I please see her?" I blurted out.

"As I just mentioned, she is in recovery, and we need to make sure her vitals stabilize." He explained with no reproach in his tone for my lack of listening. "We will come get you the moment you can see her."

He dropped my hand I had forgotten he held and with that, he took his leave.

It's funny what we think of at these moments. Ivy was somewhere in the hospital, laying lifeless, more than likely unrecognizable, and my thoughts shifted to what she had been wearing this morning. I remembered her standing in the garden talking to me in the new T-shirt she had bought with her first pay check. She was so proud of herself. Had she been wearing that when she left? Had it been destroyed? Why that added a heavier weight to my overloaded heart, I didn't know. I would buy her one in every colour when she came home.

About twenty minutes later, I was led into the room by the charge nurse. Despite the warning of how bad Ivy looked, I simply wasn't prepared for what I saw. There, in the middle of the hospital bed was my Ivy, all six feet of her looking more like four, with tubes coming from every part of her broken body. With strength I didn't know I had, I slowly approached and gently reached for her hand. I was scared to touch her, afraid I might break another bone in her already pain-riddled body.

"Ivy, baby. It's Mom. I'm here, Ivy. Can you hear me?" I prayed for some kind of acknowledgement. Some sign she heard me. A minute passed. Then two. No reply came. I felt the heat of my tears washing down my cheeks. I turned to where Dex was, and it was almost my undoing when I saw he too was crying. Until today, I had only seen him cry tears of joy, never tears of grief.

Instinctively I went to comfort him, but I was surprised when he brushed me aside. "Not now. I just can't." With that, he turned and left the room.

We handled grief in our own way, and I decided to cut him some slack for what had transpired between us. He would likely break if he took comfort from me, and we needed to be strong, especially in the room with Ivy. Still, I found it odd that at a time like this, he kept his distance, but now wasn't the time to worry about us. Ivy needed me, and I was going nowhere until she came with me.

Dexter

My life had become a runaway train, and I was powerless to stop it. Addie had seen me crying a few short minutes ago in Ivy's hospital room and wanted to comfort me, but my grief and immense guilt was too much for me to bear. I needed air. I went into the family bathroom, shut the door and fell to my knees. Holy fuck. What had I done to our family?

I wasn't a religious man. Religion was more Adalynn's thing, but I bowed my head and pleaded with God to save my little girl. I asked to change spots with her, that if she woke, I promised to be the best man I knew how to be. Ivy's image flashed through my mind. She was so swollen and broken. It was impossible for me to look at her in that condition and not feel unearthly despair and rage at how life had dealt me this hand.

A few short years ago, I had a wife I adored, children who appeared healthy and happy, and Addie and I had jobs we loved. Fast forward one short, complicated, hellish year, and I couldn't believe this was my reality. I had almost lost Seri, Ivy was facing an unthinkable battle back to us, I had no idea who my wife was and I had committed adultery.

I pleaded and bargained with God one more time and selfishly added forgiveness for myself for where I had been this morning. If forgiveness was not yet possible, at least give me strength to face Addie. I swiped the seemingly endless tears from my cheeks and got up off the floor. The only thing I could do was be there for Ivy. I would tell her that we needed her, and we wouldn't be whole without her. I did what I could to compose myself and returned to Ivy's room.

Addie was sitting beside the bed, one hand holding Ivy's, the other lovingly stroking her hair. She was singing to her.

"You are my sunshine, my only sunshine..."

The scene in front of me almost broke me. I swallowed what felt like a ball of hot lava and edged forward to the other side of the bed.

"She hasn't so much as stirred," Addie whispered to me. I think she sensed I was on the verge of collapsing and quickly added, "but the doctor said that was to be expected. She needs the rest to heal."

I had no words to offer her in return. I had no hope. It seemed my prayer had fallen on deaf ears. I couldn't even make eye contact with Addie because I would blurt out that I was sorry, and she would have no clue what I was talking about. This was not the time or place to discuss what I had done.

I was too afraid to touch Ivy in case I did more harm to her, so I pulled up a chair and stared at her swollen, bruised face. I never put much stock into "aha moments" but as I watched the ventilator breathing for her, my aha moment hammered into my chest. I felt nothing but remorse for my part in my family's demise. For my denial that Seri had ever needed professional help. That the toll of that decision I made would destroy everything Addie and I had built together. If only I had understood the daily anguish Seri had been in, the stress it put on Addie as her mother and how left out Ivy was feeling. Seeing my daughter lying in this bed could have been avoided. I would never forgive myself if Ivy didn't pull through.

Time inched forward little by little until nightfall arrived. Doctors had been in and out to check on Ivy constantly, and one nurse had stayed in the room since we had arrived. That worried me and when I asked the nurse about it, she said it was normal with patients in ICU after major surgery. It was about 10 o'clock before Addie spoke to me.

"You might as well go home, get some rest. I'll stay tonight. No sense both of us staying."

I felt like an asshole, but I didn't want to stay. I was drowning with each passing minute and didn't know if I could stay afloat much longer. The doctor who was in to check on Ivy told us her vitals were good and suggested we take turns staying with her. "One of you get some rest," he'd said, so I felt reassured enough to head home. Addie wouldn't leave first, and maybe not at all.

I leaned down and ever so gently, kissed the top of Ivy's hair. "You got this, kid. Rest up, and I'll see you tomorrow."

It wasn't until I was in the truck, driving home, that I realized I hadn't said good-bye to Addie. I hadn't even glanced in her direction. She used to say you should never leave someone mad or without a good-bye because you wouldn't want that to be the last thing said or done to someone. I had no doubt it was weighing on her mind that I had left the room and hadn't acknowledged her. Or maybe it wasn't. We hadn't been speaking much anymore. I should have learned from experience though, that life was short, and I should have acknowledged her on my way out but truthfully, I was too much of a coward to look her in the eye. I selfishly hoped she thought my grief was too consuming for me to think straight. If she knew the truth, it would devastate her. Please forgive me, Addie. I am not done breaking your already fractured heart.

July 25th, 2018

Adalynn

The night passed as slowly as I had figured it would. Ivy hadn't moved a muscle, not even an involuntary twitch, all night long. She continued to sleep, while I couldn't sleep, in part from worry, in part from anger and in part from the clock on the wall.

I made a mental note to tell someone that analog clocks should be banned from hospitals. It was agonizing enough watching your loved one suffer, but listening to and watching the second hand make its way around the clock to signal every single second was excruciating. Sixty ticks in a minute. Thirty-six hundred ticks in an hour. Tick. Tick. Tick. All night long. That was the sound. Tick. Tick. Tick. Twenty-eight thousand ticks had transpired throughout the night. It was enough to drive anyone to the brink of madness. I tried to concentrate on the vent breathing for Ivy, which absurdly reassured me because it meant my little girl was still getting the oxygen she needed. But once I had noticed the clock, it overtook my thoughts, and it was all I could hear.

Or was the clock a good thing? Was the continuous, steady ticking keeping me sane, not allowing my mind to wander? It was a safe thing to concentrate on. Count the ticks. Watch the hands move around in circles. I did not want to think of anything else. My mind never produced good thoughts when it wandered.

I was not capable of processing another crisis right now. At first I hadn't been able to comprehend why Dexter had left the room without saying good-bye. We were not on great terms but we hadn't been deliberately rude with each other. Until last night when he left. It wasn't until he leaned over to kiss Ivy goodnight that I sensed he struggled with more than his daughter in the hospital. The scent of vanilla lingered in the air. A scent I didn't use. The barely visible lipstick on the collar of his polo work shirt was a shade I would never have been bold enough to wear.

"Good morning, Mrs. Bartley. Did you get any rest?" I glanced at the nurse who had entered the room. This must have been Megan, the one taking over for Edith, who was finishing up her night shift.

"No, I didn't. I didn't expect to," I answered quietly.

Megan reached the bed and put her hand on my shoulder. "She put in a great night, I hear. Her vitals are great. She's a fighter, your girl." She turned her attention to my daughter. "Aren't you, Ivy?"

I was very much comforted by her words and her cheery disposition. Surely she wouldn't be so perky if she thought Ivy was not going to recover. My Ivy was a fighter, and I had no doubt we would be going home soon.

Megan took Ivy's temperature, checked the vitals and looked at the bandages that covered her leg, arm and head. Satisfied, she left, leaving Ivy and me alone once again.

"Morning, my beautiful girl." I raised Ivy's good arm and placed a kiss on her hand. "I hope you enjoyed your rest. I don't think you have ever been so still and quiet in your entire life." My joke did nothing to cheer me up. "Listen, Ivy, I am so, so sorry I didn't go with you yesterday. I should have been in the car with you. Maybe things would have been different. I... I know you were mad when you left, and for that I am sorry. I never thought I had to worry about you. You have always been my anchor in a stormy sea. You always have it together and never seemed to need anyone, but I was wrong."

I stopped for a moment, trying to gather my thoughts. I believed Ivy could hear me, and I had so much to say.

"I had all night to think, and I think I forgot to tell you how important you are to me, Ivy. To all of us." I gently stroked her hand. "I think so much of my time has been spent with Seri that I didn't give you the proper amount of attention. I want you to know, I am not angry at you. I'm angry at myself." I paused, making sure my emotions didn't get the best of me. "I love you more than you could ever imagine, and I'll make this up to you. I promise. You bring so much joy to my heart. You always have."

I wanted to empty out my entire well of feelings. Leave it all on the table and if Ivy could hear me, perhaps she would understand and forgive me and heal emotionally as well as physically. When I had heard the tires squealing out of our driveway, I knew she was trying to convey her hurt to me. I just didn't know how deep the hurt had run in her heart. I took another deep breath and continued talking to my little girl.

"I don't love Seri more than you, Ivy. That's not possible. The thing is, I felt like she needed me more. I felt like I was losing her, day by day to something I didn't understand. With all my might, I was trying to make her whole again. I've never looked at you like that, baby girl. I have always drawn strength from your humour, from your kind heart. Now I realize family needs each other no matter what they are battling, and that Seri's challenges were affecting you as well. I hadn't considered that, and I am so sorry I failed you." Tears spilled down my cheeks, falling onto Ivy's arm. "But if it's the last thing I do, you'll know every day for the rest of my life, just how much I love you."

When I was done talking, I felt lighter, like she was soaking in everything I was telling her. There was nothing more I could think of to say. I wiped the tears from my face and took my sleeve and gently dried Ivy's arm where the tears had travelled. It was in God's hands now. I had to wait and see what path He would lead us down.

I sat back in my chair, yawning and stretching at the same time. Checking the constantly ticking clock on the wall, I knew Dexter would be arriving soon. He had texted earlier this morning to see how Ivy was, and I had kept my answer brief: the same. He texted back to say he would be here in an hour, so I could go home, grab a shower, maybe a nap and come back. With the optimism of the nurses, I felt I had time to go home and freshen up, but I did not see much sleep in my future.

Dexter was true to his word and was at the hospital just as I stood to walk around and stretch my legs. Funny, for the first time since I had met him, I was not glad to see him. In fact, it made me sick just looking at him. I had all night to think of why there would have been lipstick on his shirt, and not one scenario played out well.

"I'll be back in an hour or so." I zipped up my purse and slung it across my shoulder.

"You don't have to rush back. I'll text if anything changes. Get some rest. You could use it."

There were times when self-control eluded me. Before I could think, I replied to him with well deserved bitterness. "How kind of you. Maybe that'll give you time to text whoever it was you were with yesterday while our child lay in a ditch." I stared directly into his eyes and took pleasure in his shocked reaction.

I didn't wait to see if he had a reply. Nothing he had to say would make this any better. I pushed past him and headed down the hall. He quickly caught up and grabbed my arm.

"Addie... I... I didn't..." The lie sat on the tip of his tongue, but he changed his mind and decided to be honest. "I don't know what to say. How did you know?" He looked like he had aged thirty years in the last minute.

"It was the lipstick. On your collar." Shame slid across his face, but it wasn't anything compared to the betrayal I felt hearing him admit that he had been with another woman. I had to give him credit. He didn't try to deny it.

"How long? How long have you been cheating on me?" This wasn't the time or place, but I needed to know. Or at least I thought I wanted to know.

"Addie, can we discuss this somewhere else?" He looked around, most likely hoping no one would hear what kind of louse he was.

"How long?" My voice was rising, and I didn't care who was in ear shot.

"We didn't sleep together. We, we didn't get the chance," he whispered and ushered me into the empty waiting room. He closed the door behind us.

"Oh, well, thank God Ivy crashed then, hey? Saved us both from a real disaster and hurt feelings," I said sarcastically. I actually hated him at this moment.

"That's not what I meant. I just meant I haven't really cheated on you. It didn't get that far." His attempt at consoling me was laughable. So laughable, in fact, I did exactly that.

"Oh, well, no hurt feelings then. You wanted to screw her but didn't get the chance. My God, I feel a thousand times better." I walked to the window and looked out. "Let me ask you something, Dex. If the roles were reversed and I had done what you did, would you consider it cheating?"

I spun around in time to see the guilt and shame on his face. He must have felt the weight of it because he collapsed into the chair and stayed silent. His silence was the only answer I needed.

With all the strength and pride I had remaining, I walked over to stand in front of him. "When I first met you, I thought I would love you forever. I never in my wildest dreams thought I would ever be capable of hating you. But I do. At this moment, I don't think I have ever hated anyone more. I hate you more than I hate myself. And that's a lot."

I opened the door and looked back before leaving the hospital. "My first and only concern is Ivy. I only ask that until we know what will happen with her, you stay away from whomever it is you are sharing your life with and stay at our house until Ivy is strong enough to come home. I can't process this right now, so I can't imagine how Seri will deal with it. It's not fair to heap separation onto the girls at this time. We can cross that bridge when Ivy is home. I hope that is something you can agree to."

Without waiting for an answer, I walked out and didn't look back, even when I heard him calling my name.

July 30th, 2018

Seraphina

I hadn't heard from The Voice in weeks. Well, to be more accurate, I was now able to silence her when she started her foolish chatter. The attempts to ambush my brain had been reduced dramatically and when it tried to overtake me, I stayed in command of my thoughts. I was winning way more battles than I was losing. Therapy had taught me several amazing techniques that made silencing my thoughts possible. I hadn't put much stock into therapy in the beginning but once I started applying the sessions to my life, things really began to change for me. It gave me a powerful feeling to be in control of my own mind. I felt liberated in ways I hadn't thought possible.

Yet, here I was longing to talk to someone even if it was myself. Strange thing for me to consider, given the fact The Voice was the reason my family was a complete disaster. It was just that this kind of silence was deafening. The house was pin-drop quiet without Ivy. It was odd not having her here with us. It felt completely wrong.

I never realized how much I loved listening to her chatter away until she wasn't capable of talking to me. She was anything but a quiet person. Boisterous, loud and hilarious were more her style. This could be accomplished without saying a word. She was like a bull moose in a China shop. Banging and crashing her way around the house, she hummed or sang to whatever was playing through her air pods. I sighed and realized I would give anything to hear her talk to me right this minute. About anything. I wouldn't even care if she started telling me ridiculous facts. She knew the most random, crazy things, like it was illegal to have a donkey sleep in your bathtub in Arizona. How this would ever be relevant to our lives didn't matter to Ivy. To her, it was pertinent that we knew these silly things. She loved sharing any bit of knowledge she came across.

It was my turn to sit with Ivy this afternoon, and it was frightening to see how still she lay in the hospital bed. Her chest barely moved up and down even with a machine doing the work. I bent closer to ensure she was still breathing. I was scared to get too close in case I hit a tube or wire, but I didn't want to be far away from her either. Making a sound or touching her let her know I was with her. She needed to know someone had been with her every single minute since she was brought to the hospital.

This was my second turn sitting with her. I hadn't spoken a word the first time I had seen her. Mom had come home after the first night to take a shower and had asked if I wanted to return to the hospital with her. I could tell by Mom's body language and tone, Ivy was not in good shape, but I needed to see for myself. I wanted to be there for my sister.

Mom was right. It was a huge shock seeing Ivy for the first time. I had no words for how it made me feel seeing a girl who was normally so full of life, my baby sister, laying deathly still in front of me. I couldn't approach the bed. From just inside the door where I had stood, the sight was ghastly enough. Bandages covered at least a third of her body and what wasn't covered, was swollen, stitched or bruised. Tubes and monitors were coming from what looked like everywhere. I was unable to move and said nothing to Ivy that first visit.

Today, however was going to be different. Today I was sitting with Ivy by myself for an hour or so, and I was determined to be a source of strength for her. Dad had to touch base with Ivan and handle company business, and Mom went home to shower and get something decent to eat. Mom was running on coffee fumes and faith, but even she needed rest. We were going on day five, and Ivy showed no signs of waking up. Her vitals were improving daily, which was a great sign, but we still had no idea the extent of her head injury. It was a positive sign, she was able to communicate before surgery, but one never knew what the human body was capable of.

I hoped I had talked Mom into getting sleep, though I doubted she would. She was afraid to leave for too long in case Ivy woke up. She wanted to be the first person Ivy saw when she opened her eyes. I understood that, so I didn't push her too hard, but she was at her breaking point, whether she admitted it or not. I was beside myself with the uncertainty of the situation and was finally getting a small taste of what it must have been like for her all these years worrying about me. It was not a pleasant feeling.

Deciding to pull my chair as close to Ivy's bed as I could, I picked it up, scooted up a few feet and quietly set it down. Repositioning myself, I bravely reached for her hand. I wasn't sure what to say or where to start, so I just dove in.

"Hey, Ives. I think you're bringing new meaning to nap time, aren't ya?" My joke was so lame, I rolled my eyes. "Yeah, so, it's clear I'm not the funny one."

The many things I wanted to say tumbled through my head, yet I didn't know where to start, so I was silent for several minutes. I wanted to tell her about Mom and Dad. They were falling apart, but that was too heavy a topic for her current state. So instead, I decided to tell her all of my favourite things. Many times, she had asked those kinds of questions, and I never really answered her. This made me sad. I knew many of Ivy's favourite things and dislikes, and not once did I ask her about any of it. She would spout these tidbits of info at me randomly, and now I clung to each fact like a lifeline. Surely God couldn't take her when she had so many favourite things here on earth. I knew her favourite color was blue, and she thought the sky had the prettiest of shades. She loved Mac and Cheese, board games that lasted for hours on a rainy day, naps, anime and random facts. She loved to make others laugh, even when she didn't feel like laughing herself.

In her mind, Chris Evans was spectacular to look at and properly built, but she hated Captain America, which always puzzled her. Shouldn't she love him too, being one and the same, she would ask. She absolutely loved to read and use her imagination. Her favourite place to read was in her room, something I had taken from her. The thought swamped me with another wave of emotion.

"You can have your room back." I stated matter-of-factly. "When you come home, all your belongings will be in your room. I promise. You can sit by the window and read. I hear there is a new series out about witches that I know you'll love. I'll pick it up today for you to read. You can tell me all about it when you're done reading." I was babbling, which was new for me. It felt strange and out of character, but I kept talking.

"My favourite color is red. I used to think it was black. I never wanted to tell you that because I was embarrassed. Black was how I saw the world. Dark, scary and not something I wanted to be a part of." As much as I was trying to reach Ivy, I was also lightening the burden that weighed heavy on my chest.

"I hate olives. I don't get the point of them. They feel weird in my mouth and taste like ass. Not that I have tasted ass, but you get my drift. I love Captain America and am not a fan of Chris Evans. More for you to puzzle over, I guess. I could play hockey every day and love being your teammate because you have a mean streak behind that gentle giant facade. I still remember you folding one girl up like an accordion for running our goalie." I chuckled out loud, thinking of that and the next thought that popped into my mind.

"Water used to be my favorite drink until the time we went for a drive, and we ran out of windshield fluid. I couldn't see with all the bugs splattered everywhere. You remember that time, Ivy?" I laughed in spite of myself. "We got a disgusting shock when I opened the water bottle and threw what was supposed to be only water onto the window. Instead, we found Christian had used it to spit his snuff into when he had gone to the beach with us the day before." I gagged at the memory, and I was suddenly aware of pressure in my hand.

"Ivy, did you just squeeze my hand?" My heart was racing, and instantly my eyes filled with tears. Hope was instantaneous at that moment. I pressed the buzzer for the nurse.

"Squeeze my hand, Ivy. Come on. You got this."

Nothing. As fast as hope had sprung into my soul, it sank like the titanic had many years before. "Please, Ivy, don't leave us. You know, when you left the day of your accident, I had a nice talk with Mom in the garden. Coincidentally, it was about you. About how much you are needed, and how little time we spend with you." Tears that had filled my eyes were slowly leaking down my cheeks. "I know you felt like I was the centre of this family. But the truth of the matter is, you are. You are the reason we pulled through every dreary day. We just didn't know it until now. We can't make it without you. I know I can't."

I fought for composure. I didn't want to burden her with any heaviness but needed to finish.

"I used to blame Mom for smothering me, you know. I could see how sad you were sometimes but at the same time, I didn't want Mom to leave my side." This was the first time I admitted that to anyone. "I needed her. Even though she had no idea how to help, she saw I was drowning, and I used her to stay afloat. I... I didn't give her the freedom she needed to be a mother to you or a wife to Dad. Be mad at me, not her, Ivy." I cupped Ivy's hand between mine and gently squeezed.

A nurse entered the room and asked why I had pressed the buzzer. She walked swiftly to the bed, and I could see she was disappointed when she realized there was no visible change in Ivy's condition.

"I thought she squeezed my hand," I stated lamely. It didn't seem as real now that the nurse was talking to Ivy while checking her over. I let go of Ivy, stood and paced at the foot of the bed.

"Perhaps she did," said the nurse, not wanting to burst my bubble. Her not dismissing the possibility gave me a good sign that maybe Ivy would stir soon. She spoke softly to Ivy while taking her blood pressure, then tested her reflexes.

Nothing.

She asked Ivy to squeeze her hand. Still nothing.

"Well, she's holding strong, but I am not getting a response right now. If it happens again, don't hesitate to buzz for someone. I'm going to note this in her chart and let the doctor know."

With that, she came to the end of the bed, reached out to touch my shoulder to show support, and then left the room.

I watched her until she disappeared down the hall. How did they do what they did every single day, I had no idea, but I appreciated hospital staff more now than when I had been here myself.

I didn't want to look at my sister. I was half mad she didn't want to wake up. Hoping that it was my voice she had responded to, I sat down and started talking again.

"I finally understand how Mom must have felt all these years. Frig. Why does life have to kick us in the ass for us to learn these lessons, Ivy?" I ran my hands through my hair. "As I watch you lay here, so quiet, it spooks me. My every thought is consumed with you. I can't concentrate on anything else. And I am scared." I paused to choke down a sob. She didn't need to hear me cry. When I thought I could hold the sobs at bay, I finished what I wanted to say.

"I'm terrified you will never get to know how much I love you, cause I sure do. I would give anything to hear another one of your crazy facts. Come on, Ivy, can you hear me? Please, don't you dare leave this world until you know how important you are in it."

There. My feelings were out in the open. I had told her everything I needed her to hear. It was up to her now to fight. "Now, enough with the nap. Wake up, and you can do some of the talking. It must be weird listening to me ramble on."

I let go of her hand, sat back in my chair and stared intently at her, willing a response. I contemplated telling her some exciting news about what had been happening between Ivan and me (she would get a kick out of me drooling over a guy) to see if that would get her attention, but a noise at the door made me turn in time to see Dad wipe at something on his cheek.

"Hey, Dad, I didn't see you there." I stood and walked over to give him a hug. I was not sure who was in need of the hug more: Dad or me, but we both held on tightly. "Work all good?" I couldn't think of anything else to say. I thought of telling him about Ivy's hand trying to squeeze mine but with each passing minute, it felt more like a figment of my imagination.

"Work's fine. Ivan is really stepping up for me," he said and moved closer to the bed. "How is she doing today?" His voice was barely more than a cracked whisper.

I hated seeing him this broken. I decided to tell him what I thought had happened.

His face lit up. "Did you tell the doctor? What did they say? This must be a good sign!"

I instantly regretted giving him so much hope. He was practically bouncing around the bed.

"A nurse came in and didn't see any visible signs of change."

His shoulders drooped once more. I kept talking.

"I didn't imagine it. I was telling Ivy a funny story, and I swear she was reacting to it."

He turned and studied my face for a minute, and then smiled. "I believe you, kiddo. Our Ivy is a fighter. Aren't you, kid?"

The room felt awkward now that Dad was here. We had no idea what to say to each other.

I noticed Mom and him weren't speaking or even sleeping in the same room, and I wanted to ask him about that but knew this was not the place. Small talk didn't seem appropriate, and my emotions were all over the place, so I didn't want to talk in case something triggered another crying jag.

"I think I'll head out now, if that's okay. I'll give you time with Ivy before Mom comes back."

He was already sitting in my spot, and his focus was clearly on Ivy. I leaned over and placed a kiss gently on his cheek. "We will be a family again, Dad. If faith has taught me anything, it's that God will help carry us through the storm. And storms never last forever."

I leaned down and placed a kiss on Ivy's head and silently prayed this storm would pass before we all ended up on different shores in its aftermath.

Dexter

The sun was shining as brightly as I had ever seen it. For some strange reason, it annoyed me that it wasn't raining. It would have been more fitting for the situation our family was in. I was barely getting by, and the sun was rubbing salt into my wounds by shining brightness over my dreary life. It was hard to wallow and lick my wounds on a sunny day.

I was sitting outside the hospital in the courtyard for patients and their families. The hospital was a children's hospital and when it was built, brightening a child's spirit was definitely at the forefront of each part of the planning stages. The gardens that outlined the courtyard and wove around each sitting area were beautiful. Every flower imaginable was in full bloom, and it looked like something I would see in a magazine or painting. Shrubs eight feet high ran through the courtyard like a maze, separating tables and benches to give families a feeling of privacy. I could hear bits of conversations, but people couldn't stare at the sick children who were well enough to venture out into the sunshine. It eliminated pity stares and gave families a bit of normalcy during an abnormal and shitty time in their lives. My thoughts drifted to Adalynn and how much joy this area would bring to her under different circumstances. I could picture the old Addie gasping at the splendour of this remarkable garden. I wondered if she had been here at any point since Ivy was brought in. She likely wouldn't have noticed its beauty even if she had. She hadn't been enjoying her own garden much these days.

It had been an incredibly long five days. I really had no idea what to do with myself. I couldn't work. The idea of building new things didn't generate joy. The thoughts of being anywhere except here at the hospital with things so uncertain didn't sit right with me either. Ivan was doing a great job of holding down the fort. An incredible job actually, so I had nothing to worry about work wise. Seri had taken it upon herself to stop by my office and check in with Ivan to see how things were going. She even offered to help with the books that I usually did, and I was seriously considering giving her the opportunity. Ivan wasn't a paperwork kind of guy, and it was the first real job Seri had taken any interest in. When I checked in yesterday, Ivan told me how big of a help Seri was. If my life wasn't such a shit show, I likely would have picked up on Ivan's tone when talking about Seri. It was the same way I used to talk about Addie. With admiration and interest. It didn't register with me, as I was having trouble focusing on anything but Ivy and why she wouldn't wake up.

I wanted to sit with Ivy every single moment until she woke, but I couldn't be in the room when Adalynn was there. We spoke not a word when we were together. There was too much tension between us, and we didn't want Ivy to pick up on that. We were convinced she could hear us, and the doctors said that while there was no way to know, they encouraged us to speak as if she could. We agreed to take shifts and avoid being in the room together. That left going home for me when it wasn't my turn, but I didn't want to be home. Home was filled with too many memories, good and bad.

The good memories were unattainable, and the barrage of bad memories wouldn't let up. I didn't need to be home to make my mind spin more than it did. It was so unnaturally quiet with no one home. I think that's what hit me the hardest: the eerie silence. Our house was once full of laughter and stories and a family who loved one another. Every room held memories that echoed around in my thoughts. I couldn't stand it.

Seri was never home anymore, which a week ago would have been cause to celebrate. Now it only made the house sadder. She was handling things much better than I thought she would, spending most of her time at Mari's or at my office helping out. Her therapist had been good to her this last week and had met with her three of the five days Ivy was in the hospital. Denise had no desire to see Seri backslide, and my gratitude for her help was overwhelming. It still pissed me off that I took so long to see the value in therapy.

In a weird, ironic way, it was nice not having Adalynn worrying so much about Seri. Although the harsh reality of why she wasn't worrying was no better a boat to be floating in on this stormy sea.

That left the courtyard for me to come sit, relax and recharge. I had only been here a handful of times, and I was struck by its peacefulness and beauty. I seemed more relaxed here than any place else. Likely because I had no memories connected to this place to assault me.

The phone in my pocket vibrated, startling me. I quickly pulled it out to see if it was news about Ivy. It was not. It was a call from Sylvia, who I hadn't seen or spoken to since I had left her house that day. She was calling to see how Ivy was, but I had no desire to talk to her. On the fifth ring, she gave up but sent me a text.

Dexter, can you please answer. We should really talk. I am worried about you.

When had I become a coward? I didn't know, but I simply couldn't face Sylvia. She was a wonderful person, but I couldn't look her in the eye and tell her what I had to say. It had been intimacy and friendship I was craving and not so much her the past few months. I had racked my brain for the last five days and for the life of me, I couldn't think of one thing about Sylvia I liked that could have built a solid foundation for a good relationship. We were completely different. She didn't want a family; I loved mine and would die for them. She didn't believe in God; I had faith even though I hadn't been to church in years. I loved staying home; she was happiest travelling the world.

What struck me the most was that everything I liked about Sylvia were the same traits Addie possessed.

The one thing I really enjoyed was talking to someone again. Laughing once more and having no serious conversations. Just hanging out and shooting the shit. I wondered if I would have strayed with anyone who had shown interest in me. Or did I really have feelings for Sylvia, and I was lying to myself? There was one way to find out. I dialed Sylvia's number. She answered on the second ring.

"Dex, how are you? I have been so worried. How is Ivy?"

At the sound of her voice, life came into perspective at lightning speed. I did not have any type of loving feelings for her. This was just a voice on the other end of my phone. I did not feel any emotions other than indifference and guilt as I replied.

"She's the same. Thanks for asking." A long awkward pause followed.

"Listen, Dex, what happened between us..."

More silence. I had to find the right words. I wasn't accustomed to hurting people, but it seemed to be my speciality lately.

"What happened between us, Sylvia, was a mistake." There was no easy way to put what I had to say. "Nothing should have ever happened. I think I was..."

"Lonely?" She finished my sentence accurately. I was surprised she was so understanding.

"Yes. I was lonely. I enjoyed talking about everything and nothing. I didn't feel like I was failing with you, if that makes any sense. My home life was falling apart, and this gave me an escape from it. I never talked to you about my family, or what we were going through. I felt like if I did, that would have been cheating on Addie." I scoffed at how dumb that sounded, but Sylvia seemed to get it.

"I never pushed you to. I know how much you love her and your girls." She paused, waiting for me to continue. She was trying to understand her part in all this. What part of my life she fit into.

"It's no excuse for what almost happened. What did happen." I ran my hand through my hair as I continued to speak. "I owe you an explanation as to why I did what I did." I paused, searching for the right words. "I missed talking to my wife. We've had a hell of a year. I never told you about our oldest daughter and her struggles, but it was rough for a long time. I didn't know how to deal with it. I sound like a complete asshole saying this out loud, but I really didn't get what Seri's issues were. I pretended we had perfect kids and a perfect marriage, and I had buried my head in the sand and ignored how badly my family was suffering. Things slowly changed with Addie, and I felt like I didn't matter to her anymore. When I started your renovation, and we got to talking, well..." Again I tried finding appropriate words. Words that would not hurt Sylvia but not lead her on either. "You made me feel wanted. I didn't have to deal with the everyday with you. We could just talk. I hadn't felt that in a long time. Loneliness is a dangerous feeling."

"I get lonely too. I have no family and although that's because I don't want one, I enjoyed our talks. It's been a long time since I shared my heart with someone. I wasn't expecting to enjoy your company so much. You became important to me quicker than I realized. One thing led to another and," she spoke the next part quietly, "I fell for you."

I didn't know how to reply. There was a part of me that wanted to tell her she mattered to me. She had been my friend and confidant when I was at my lowest. But a bigger part of me knew that if I comforted this woman, it might open the door to hope.

It would also be another stab in Adalynn's back. To soothe and care for another woman wasn't in my marriage vows. I had no interest in hurting Addie ever again. Whether or not she and I weathered this storm, I was not going to be intentionally responsible for any more of her heartache.

"I don't want to hurt you, Sylvia." This was proving to be more emotional than I wanted it to be. "But I love Adalynn. She's the only woman I have ever loved and if she'll still have me, I want to save my marriage."

"She doesn't have to know about us. I won't ever say anything. Can we talk in person, at least before final decisions are made? Don't you owe me this?"

Desperation filled Sylvia's voice. An emotion I didn't know she was capable of. She was always so sure of herself. I thought she was not one to emotionally attach to someone, which only made me feel like a bigger asshole. I thought she understood I wanted no complications. Another prick thing for me to be thinking.

"She knows about us. Well, she knows that I was with someone the day Ivy..." I couldn't finish that sentence. "That's all I have thought about besides Ivy these past five days. How much I hurt my wife. It kills me that I did this to her. Even though we didn't sleep together, I still betrayed the woman I promised never to hurt."

"What about what this is doing to me? My feelings don't matter? Nothing we have matters?" Her voice was rising, and I was stunned at the emotion she was showing. I hated she felt this way, but I hated the sadness I saw in Addie more. I mentally berated myself again and pushed through this hard conversation.

"I never meant to hurt you." How feeble and cliché was that, but it was true. "But I won't be seeing you anymore."

It took a moment for her to respond. "I see. So, this is it? Just, oops, sorry I used you but screw off? We can't even discuss this in person like real adults?" Hope resonated in her voice behind the sarcasm and anger. She was hoping that maybe I would relent and see her.

"There's nothing left to say. I'm truly sorry." I remembered the reason I had met Sylvia in the first place and added, "I'll get Ivan to finish up at your house, or I can get another contractor over." I wanted to see her project finished. She deserved that much from me.

Sylvia let out a humourless laugh. "I can handle things from here. I don't need you or your help. I'll send what I feel I owe you to your office." Her tone changed, and she sounded business like and much colder.

"Listen, don't worry about the bill. It's on me." I was fumbling for the right way to end this part of my life.

She softened her tone when she next spoke. "I don't want anything from you, but I appreciate the offer. I want to thank you for the job you did. It's beautiful. Good-bye, Dex. I hope your daughter pulls through."

She hung up before I could say anything else. It was just as well. I had said all I wanted to say.

Well, fuck. I let out a huge sigh and put my phone away. I thought I heard someone crying close by, and my heart went out to them. I hoped it wasn't bad news about their child. Whatever had brought on their tears, I knew their pain. Life for anyone in this courtyard wasn't what they hoped for. I felt a strange pull to the sound. I gave serious thought about making my way to their section and offering... what? My tank was empty, and I had nothing left to offer anyone. Besides, they would likely be embarrassed if I intruded on their privacy.

I got up off the bench and stretched my legs. My heart felt like it was in conflicting states. It was heavier, yet much lighter at the same time. I knew in my heart, I would never cheat on Addie again. Ever. There were too many people who got hurt. Sylvia wasn't an innocent party and had known I was married, but it didn't make knowing she was hurting any less real to me. The girls would be devastated when they found out. It would open the wound all over again when it was time to tell them and most likely cause irrevocable damage in our relationships too. But I felt lighter knowing I had taken responsibility for what I had done and was honestly willing to learn from this. It was Addie I wanted. I hoped I had the chance to prove to her I was a man she could trust again, but I had a bad feeling I'd never get that shot.

Regardless of what happened with Addie, for my sake, I wanted to be a better man. I had left two women heartbroken in the wake of my bad choices. I had allowed myself to be selfish. A family man couldn't afford that luxury. At least that's what I had told Addie on our wedding day. I had looked her in the eye and told her that no matter what happened in our future, I promised to consider her in every decision. I had shattered that promise and would spend the rest of my life trying to make amends.

No longer able to sit and relax, I decided to walk up to Ivy's room and see how my girls were doing. With any luck, or small miracle, Ivy would be awake.

By the time I approached Ivy's room, I had put the whole Sylvia part of my life behind me. I was only going to look forward from here. No good would come from dwelling on things I couldn't change. As I reached the doorway, I heard Seri talking to Ivy. I quietly slid inside the door, and the sight of Seri holding Ivy's hand was enough to bring tears to my eyes. The next words Seri spoke, made those tears spill over.

"I finally understand how Mom must have felt all these years. Frig. Why does life have to kick us in the ass for us to learn lessons, Ivy?"

Seri's words made a big impact on me. We were getting a taste of the constant worry Addie had been feeling for the past year. My angst since I had laid eyes on Ivy had been never ending. I couldn't eat, sleep or even think straight. I felt like I had jumped out of a plane, and I was spiralling down to the earth at break-neck speed, but my chute refused to open. Thoughts consumed me. How useless I was for Ivy as she battled for her life, fearing the outcome would not be in her favour and trying to bargain with God to bring her back to us. It shamed me to admit, I never felt like that when Seri had been struggling with her mental health. I couldn't see Seri's illness, so I didn't think of it as a real problem. It was a horrifying revelation.

Addie saw our daughter's pain. She saw the mental anguish Seri was struggling with, and, day by day, it had eaten away at her. Compounded with the fact that I couldn't see it, or rather wouldn't acknowledge it, Addie had changed. I had changed Addie.

Seri was still talking. She had lowered her voice, so I moved closer to hear.

"Please, don't you dare leave this world until you know how important you are in it." She paused. I think she was trying to regain her composure and make the conversation lighter.

I had never said those words to Seri. Not even during her deepest, darkest moments. I hadn't told her what she had meant to me, to her family. I let her suffer in silence, content in my negligent disregard and ignorance. I couldn't, rather wouldn't, admit that something could be wrong with my little girl. Guilt was the most dominate emotion that hammered me. A lump formed in my throat.

Seri let go of Ivy's hand, sat back in her chair and sighed. She looked completely spent. Before moving deeper into the room, I wiped at my face to erase any evidence of tears. I cleared my throat, and the noise reached Seri. She turned to see who was behind her.

"Hey, Dad, I didn't see you there." She came over and gave me a hug. I should have taken this moment to tell her what was in my heart. Let her know how much she meant to me but instead, I clung to her. I hoped she could feel what was in my heart. I loved her with all of my being.

"Work all good?"

I told her things were fine, and her next words raised my spirits for the first time in what seemed like years.

"I think I felt Ivy squeeze my hand."

Hope surged through me but when I asked her what happened next, it was clear she was the only one who had witnessed the event. I stared at her for a moment. My first reaction was disbelief. According to her, the nurse hadn't seen any intentional movements, nor had I since I had entered the room. She was likely misinterpreting an involuntary twitch. We had been warned about those. Yet, when I looked into Seri's eyes, I saw truth. I saw a girl needing her dad to believe her, and I wasn't going to let her down this time. Just because I didn't see Ivy move, didn't mean it hadn't happened.

"I believe you, kiddo." I turned to look at Ivy. "Our Ivy is a fighter. Aren't you, kid?"

We both fell silent, and I was trying to think of a way to tell Seri I had failed her. I needed her to know my part in all of this was likely the catalyst that sent our family into a tailspin. I just didn't want to do it in front of Ivy.

It was Seri who broke the silence. She decided to take off. She gave both Ivy and I a kiss, spoke some reassuring words and left. I made my way to the chair that sat diligently beside Ivy. I gingerly reached for her hand, as Seri had done, and touched it briefly to my lips.

"Hey, baby girl. Seri said you had a trick to show me," I began. "When you think I have reached your humour level, give me two squeezes, okay? Did you hear the one about the man who stole all the farmer's eggs?"

And with that, I talked to Ivy non-stop until Adalynn showed up a little while later.

Adalynn

It was odd to be outside and not in my garden. I closed my eyes and recalled the state of my backyard haven. The vegetables were starting to rebel and wither against my neglect, but I couldn't muster the strength to care. I had no desire to see the beauty in anything that was growing healthy and vibrant while my baby was fighting for her life.

A few friends had offered to make sure the weeds didn't take over and for once, I didn't fight the help. I reduced the store hours to what worked for them and surprisingly, business stayed steady. I couldn't remember the last time I had let someone into my domain and touch anything in my garden, but I was certainly grateful to have one less worry on my plate. I spotted Seri in the garden a few times, and it did my heart wonders seeing her holding up so well. I felt guilty that my attention had shifted so dramatically from Seri to Ivy, but a mamma bear couldn't watch one of her cubs in peril and shrug it off.

Part of me was enjoying this new-found freedom when it came to Seri. Although it had been less than a week since I stopped hovering over her, it seemed like she didn't need me to be around her at all times. I used to feel like even though she hated me constantly in sight, she needed that. Like I was her life jacket on a sinking boat. Or perhaps I only felt like Seri was doing well because all my energy was being poured into Ivy, and I didn't want to feel guilty. I didn't think that was the case though. I made sure to touch base with Seri every day, and she was helping in any way she could. She had done more for us in five days than she had in her entire lifetime, and I couldn't have been prouder. Her time was split between Mari's house and Dexter's office. She mentioned to me several times how great Ivan was, and I wasn't sure if she was showing interest or gratitude for how he was handling the business for Dexter. Either way, it did my heart good to see she was trying. Therapy had been a godsend. The only bad thing I could say was, Seri had picked up on the tension between Dexter and me, but she only inquired about it once. I told her we all handled stress differently, and we would get through this as a family and for her not to worry. I only hoped she believed me when I told her that lie.

Shading my eyes, I took a good look at my surroundings. I was walking in one of the most beautiful areas of the hospital. It was a courtyard designed to give families privacy, but also make them feel like they were in a little slice of heaven while going through hell. Under different circumstances, I would have marvelled at the garden design and extraordinary arrangement of shrubbery and flowers but instead, I was grateful for the solitude the shrubbery offered. This was my third time here. I closed my eyes and imagined myself telling Ivy and Seri the name of every flower the next time I visited. It was a wonderful thought and a bit depressing. Try as I might, all my thoughts of the future no longer included Dexter. I tried to shove him from my mind, but he kept pushing his way into my thoughts. It was like I could hear him talking. Or was that actually him?

I crept to the bench situated to the back of my section and leaned towards the sound of the voice. It was Dexter talking. I couldn't hear anyone else, so I assumed he was on the phone. He had a voice that carried like a megaphone. Ivy was just like him in that regard. I heard them before I saw them. He was chatting with Ivan, I guessed. It was work-related talk. His voice aroused my hurt and anger but also my longing for him to wrap his arms around me and tell me this was a bad dream, and we would be waking soon, together.

He ended the call with Ivan, and I wondered what he was thinking. Was he thinking of me? Did he miss me at all, or were his thoughts on his bimbo? Were they in love? Were they sleeping together? I tried to put him out of my mind and flipped open the journal I had been writing in. Needing something to do while waiting for my turn to see Ivy each day, I had decided to chronicle my life to date. I was detailing the good and the bad that had led me to this point. Seri had suggested journal writing, having learned about it in therapy. She wasn't a writer, but she knew I dabbled in it and thought I would benefit.

She wasn't wrong. I would write a while longer before I went up to see the girls. This was only Seri's second time with Ivy, and I didn't want to intrude. The girls needed their time together.

I was almost a full page into writing down my sordid thoughts when what sounded like Dexter's phone, rang. He didn't answer. Was it his new woman? Someone needing work? I closed the journal and put both the pen and the writing pad into my purse. I would only write mean-spirited things in this mood, and that wasn't what I wanted to do. I wanted to give this journal to my girls eventually, so they could understand what they both meant to me, and why I had made the choices I had in my life. They didn't need to read a chapter on how much I wanted to chop off their father's organ and use it as compost in my garden.

I decided to head up to Ivy's floor and wait in the family room so I wouldn't have to wonder who was or wasn't calling my lousy husband. The view wasn't as pretty, but it was farther away from him. As I got up to leave, I heard him speak.

"She's the same. Thanks for asking."

Two things I knew at this moment. The first, Dex must have called the person he was talking to. I hadn't heard his phone ring again. Secondly, they were asking how Ivy was. I stayed as still and as quiet as I could. My gut was telling me this was the woman who had stolen my husband's heart. I needed to know how he spoke to her. Was he happy when he heard her voice? Was he still seeing her? I sat down, closed my eyes and continued to eavesdrop.

"What happened between us, Sylvia, was a mistake." His voice was concise and to the point. "Nothing should have ever happened. I think I was..." and then silence.

My blood rushed to my face, and I nearly passed out from the speed of it. I grabbed the back of the bench in an effort to steady myself. Sylvia. That was her name. The woman who Dexter had shared some of his life with. The overwhelming feeling of nausea made me gag. I plugged my ears and rocked slowly back and forth. While I didn't want to hear any more, I couldn't pull myself away. I decided this might be the only time I heard the truth of what was happening between Dexter and his fling. Unplugging my ears, I tilted my head towards the conversation.

"My home life was falling apart, and this gave me an escape from it. I never talked to you about my family, or what we were going through. I felt like if I did, that would have been cheating on Addie."

The pressure around my heart eased with those words. He had kept his family to himself. I don't know why, but that mattered to me. I wished I could hear Sylvia's side of this conversation, but I settled for what I could hear.

Dex poured out his heart to this stranger, and I felt like none of it was real. I felt like I was having an out-of-body experience as I listened to him tell another woman about me. About my daughter. Confessing that loneliness had driven him to do what he had done. A slice of guilt shot through me. What he was saying about me not being there for him wasn't wrong. In fact it was painfully accurate. When was the last time he and I had sat down and watched a sunset on the back deck? Or taken a drive to see construction projects he had completed. I remembered the night we had made love on the deck, and then I brushed him off like dust on my overalls. That had been the last time we were intimate. Every time I told him I was too busy or too worried was equivalent to pushing him one step closer to this woman. I cried so often now, I let the tears that had been threatening fall where they may.

"I don't want to hurt you, Sylvia. But I love Adalynn. She's the only woman I have ever loved and if she'll still have me, I want to save my marriage."

Oh, Dexter. The sobs overtook me. I did my best to cry as quietly as I could. I didn't need or want anyone wandering over to see my grief. Especially Dexter. I would have been mortified if he knew I was listening in. His words echoed in my ears. He still loved me. I was the only woman he had ever loved. Could that be true? He had no idea I was listening, which again reinforced my hopes he sincerely meant what he was saying. He had no reason to lie while talking to her and the words I was hearing now, strangely meant more to me than if he was telling me this to my face. He told Sylvia flat out they were not going to see each other anymore. I took comfort in those words but each time I closed my eyes, all I could picture was him in the arms of another woman. It was a hard image to erase.

From their conversation, I knew they hadn't slept together but just knowing it was Ivy's accident that prevented them from screwing, didn't sit well with me. I looked up to the sky for answers. Was I supposed to believe that Ivy's accident was God's way of saving our marriage by stopping Dexter from making the biggest mistake of his life? But why use Ivy in such a drastic way? The more I thought about my life, the more I realized that in the last five days, things for our family were shifting. Seri was no longer first thing on my mind. She was growing into a confident, kind and beautiful young woman. I was seeing her the way she wanted me to see her since her suicide attempt over four months ago. She was strong and on her way to being fully independent. Not the feeble, insecure girl she was before her intense therapy. I hadn't seen that until Ivy needed me.

Because of this accident, Dexter realized his shortcomings in Seri's life. I heard the regret wrapped around every word he spoke to Sylvia. We both let Seri down for years. I wasn't blameless in Dexter reaching out to another woman. People need intimacy. We all need someone we can talk to. To hold. I hadn't been that person for him for almost a year. No, I hadn't strayed, but I had been laser-focused on Seri and no one else, another unhealthy relationship for both of us.

Then there was Ivy. My comedic, kind-hearted, gentle giant. She had been invisible to me for years, and I hadn't realized what

I was doing to her. Now I knew Ivy was the glue that held us together and unbeknownst to her, she was the reason our family was going to survive this.

For the first time since Ivy was brought in, I considered the higher purpose of her accident. And I was filled with hope. Hope that we could learn from these hard lessons and come out the family we used to be. Hope that I could tell Dexter, in time, I forgive him and really mean it. Hope that Ivy would wake up soon, and I could tell her how much she meant to me, to all of us. I knew the road wasn't going to be easy but for the first time in a very long time, my heart held genuine hope.

I held nothing back, letting myself cry until I simply couldn't anymore. I tried being strong, stifling my emotions, but it was time I let them out. By the time I was done, I felt tired but satisfied. I can't say why hope was a feeling I had at this point, but it's no different from faith, and I still had that. I put my hands together, said a quick prayer and up to the fifth floor I went.

The first person I saw was Dexter sitting beside Ivy, telling what sounded like terrible dad jokes. I smiled in spite of myself. The jokes hadn't disturbed Ivy. She was resting peacefully. I told myself she needed a bit more rest before she returned to us, then I bravely entered the room. Dexter turned when he saw me approaching and for the first time since I saw the lipstick on his collar, I didn't feel rage in my heart. I felt hope continuing to grow. Our eyes locked, and I saw his silent plea.

At this moment, I had a choice to make. I could offer up my forgiveness and walk the bumpy road with him or stay laced in bitterness and walk the road alone. The choice was the hardest one I would ever make.

I finished walking to where he sat. His back was to me again, and he hit Ivy with the punch line of his joke. His voice cracked from emotion. I rested my hand on his shoulder, and he stopped mid-sentence and faced me. The emotion in his expression was blinding.

When I spoke, I felt like I had never said truer words. "Lucky for us, you won't have to tell the jokes much longer. Ivy is going to take that job back. Aren't you, Ives? We're all going to be okay."

He covered my hand with his. I felt the warmth of his body, saw the love in his eyes and knew we were heading in the right direction.

Ivy

I heard them talking. Not every single word, but most of them. I had no recollection of what had happened, or where I was. All I knew for certain was I was exhausted. I didn't feel pain so much as fatigue. I had never felt this kind of tired in my entire life. I slept way more than I was awake, which should have delighted me but instead, I found it getting old.

For the first little while, I couldn't distinguish who was talking. Then, as my brain fog cleared, it became obvious to me that I may be in a hospital. I heard the word vitals a lot, and sometimes I felt pokes in different places on my body.

Someone kept banging on my knees and elbows and when I finally escaped this nap, I had every intention of returning the favour and whacking them in their sleep. After every nap, I felt stronger. Although the more alert I became, the more I realized I might have been run over by a dump truck full of heavy boulders. Pain radiated from everywhere. I assumed medicine eased it at times, and I took advantage of the relief when it came and slept.

I had just woken again from a long winter's nap (I couldn't remember if it was winter or summer), and the voice I heard was my dad's. I concentrated hard and tried to hear what he was saying. Something about a farmer and eggs. Oh no, he was trying to be funny, wasn't he? Poor guy. I needed to get back to my family, if only so no one was subjected to his jokes.

How long had I been lying here? I tried to lift my arms, but I didn't feel like I was attached to them. It was hard to describe, but I felt like I was bodiless, more of an entity. Not like I was floating around the room or anything like I had seen in movies. It was harder to describe than that. It was like I was telling my brain to do something, and it was full out ignoring me. Again, I tried to move, but this time I thought I would have better luck with my eyes. I went to take a deep breath and realized something: I wasn't breathing on my own! Well, that seemed bad. Was I actually dead? Did a lot of people die the same day I did, and was I put in this deep sleep to await my turn for judgement?

Damn. This wasn't good.

But, if I was dead, what was with all the vital talk and swinging hammers at my knees and elbows? No, I was alive. I must have been hooked up to a vent to do my breathing for me. Maybe I was in a coma. I had seen that on shows and never gave it much thought, but this must be what was going on. Why else couldn't I move? If things weren't so hazy, I might have been scared. I lost my train of thought. What had I been doing? Oh, right, sleeping.

I dozed off again. For how long, I had no idea but when I came around again, Dad was still spitting out jokes. Good grief. He was keeping me in this state, I was sure of it.

"Do you know why I took an extra pair of socks to the golf course, Ivy... In case I got a hole in one!" I thought I heard a little chuckle from someone. Had it been me? Or Dad? Nobody should be chuckling at that.

Darkness overtook me, and I faded off to sleep once more. This time when I woke, I heard Seri talking. She was begging me to come back to her. Hmmm. This was a nice change. A little bit of me time. I liked how this was shaping up. I tried to listen harder, but she seemed a million miles away.

She was telling me about the time we threw spit and snot, or as she called it, snuff onto the window of our car. Now that had been funny. But as she told the funny story, I didn't like how worried she sounded between her laughter. I wanted to tell her I was trying to wake up from this incredibly long and stubborn nap. My hand was wedged between hers. I mustered up all my will power and energy I had. Come on, come on... I can do this.

"Ivy, did you just squeeze my hand?"

Why yes, yes, I did. Could she hear me, or was that only in my head? She begged me to move again. Try as I might, I was just too tired. I couldn't concentrate on what she was saying. I fought the abyss that was sucking me back in.

Her words were so kind. So kind, it was a bit creepy. Yip. I was dying. No way she would be telling me this stuff otherwise. I didn't want to die yet cause if I heard right, I was getting my room back, and I had a really good book to finish.

I succumbed to the darkness. For how long this time, I had no way of knowing. What I did know was, I woke to the sadist who enjoyed poking me and causing me pain. Damn, I think they stuck me with a needle in my shin this time. Kneecap battery wasn't enough? Things were getting violent out there. I wanted to kick back at my attacker, but my body was just too lazy.

Each time I woke, things were getting clearer to me. I was definitely in the hospital. My parents and Seri hadn't left my side since I had arrived. They were constantly telling me they loved me. I had to wake up soon, if for no other reason than to tell them it wasn't just me who could talk a person's ear off. These guys were nonstop jabbering at me. It was nice, but a bit overwhelming.

I had no memory of how I got here, but I understood it was time for me to wake up. It was the pain that held me back. If I was sleeping, I couldn't feel anything.

Wow.

Wasn't that what Seri had said to me a long time ago? Memories flooded me all at once, and I remembered being mad at Mom.

Something about Seri. Oh, yeah. I had felt left out. I was mad at Seri too. It was harder to remember why, but I think it was because I didn't believe she was hurting. I understood her more now. I was trying to make my brain listen to me and wake up, but it was doing its own thing. Is this the kind of struggle she faced? If so, she must have felt so alone. Like I did now. I heard my family, but they couldn't help me. This was something I was going to have to do on my own, and the task of waking up seemed too daunting.

Well, by golly, I was going to wake up right this minute. I was pretty sure I heard Mom asking, or maybe she was telling me things were going to be okay. A perfect time to show her she was right. She always liked it when her motherly instincts were on point. I would give her the credit for my timely awakening, even if it was me doing all the work. I decided to try my eyes again. They felt weighed down, but not to the same extreme that my arms felt. I concentrated as best I could. Move... move... My eyelids didn't open, but I felt my eyeballs shifting around. Okay. This was good. I cleared my mind and tried again. My eyelids must have been opening because light was piercing my skull. Ew. Not as exciting as I had imagined, but I wasn't going to let a little pain stop me. I had come this far. Darn it, I was going to open my eyes. I heard Mom in my head telling me to fight and as my eyelids slowly rose and my eyes adjusted to the brightness, I realized Mom and Dad were sitting beside me. Mom was the one doing the talking. I could feel more than see their excitement.

"Welcome back, Ivy. We love you."

There. I did it. I showed them I wasn't dead. The corners of my mouth responded to the fact I was trying to smile. I would take a little rest and then maybe next time I came around, I would tell Dad a joke cause his really were terrible.

August 20th, 2032

Dexter

"Hurry up, folks," I yelled from the kitchen. "I don't want to be late! Cake is always at 6 pm sharp!" I placed the birthday cake in a container, then I put plastic utensils and paper plates into a bag.

"Don't get your knickers in a bunch," said Ivy. "We're a coming!"

I smiled. I never got sick of the sound of her voice no matter what she was saying. She was thirty years old now, but I could still see her lying in that hospital bed like it was yesterday. It had taken her five days to wake up and another twenty-two days to be well enough to come home to us. Incredibly, her brain function returned to normal. For the first month or so, she mixed up a lot of her words but eventually, that went away. Physical therapy had lasted much longer. Other than a slight limp, there were no lasting visible scars from her accident.

From the moment she had stepped back into our house, it felt like a home again. We were able to pick up the pieces from our shattered life and rebuild what we had lost. It was like doing a thousand-piece jigsaw puzzle that we slowly but surely completed.

Addie's relationship with both girls flourished, and the laughter returned to our home. Ivy harboured no hard feelings and soaked up the attention we lavished on her while she was healing. Adalynn stopped fretting over both girls soon after Ivy was up walking, and her attention began to centre around her own life and our fragile relationship.

I don't know what had transpired in Adalynn's life that motivated her to forgive me so easily. That day in the hospital, when Ivy came back to us, I knew our family was going to be okay. When Addie had laid her hand on my shoulder, it was the first step towards our reconciliation. A month after Ivy had come home, Addie and I had a long, meaningful talk. She told me all her regrets, feelings, insecurities and hopes for the future. She offered me an apology and told me the most important thing to her was family. I did the same. I wanted to explain why I had strayed, but she quietly told me it didn't matter. She had all the answers she needed on the subject, and she never wanted the girls to know. She didn't want them to think less of me. I was touched and humbled by that. Sylvia was never mentioned again. I did, however, promise her that for the rest of our lives, I would never hurt her like that again.

It was a promise I had kept. I had wondered from time to time why she had let my indiscretion go so easily, but she was content to leave the past in the past. When Ivy was back to herself and didn't need our help anymore, Addie and I decided to travel and rekindle our romance and adventurous nature. The girls loved the idea of us not being around all the time, and they loved helping with Addie's business and mine. Ivy fell in love with gardening, and Seri was better at handling my books and appointments than I was. We took full advantage of our second chance and saw nine countries in Europe, followed by an Alaskan cruise. It was the happiest we had been in years. I had found my best friend again.

It took time, but Addie let me back into her bed. I never pushed her, and I understood she would have to be the one who initiated sex. At first, she was timid. I could only imagine what was running through her mind. While I was determined to be patient, I wanted to show her how much I desired her. I was not able to control myself the third time we attempted to make love, and I accidentally ripped her shirt in my haste to devour her. After that, her inhibitions disappeared, and we couldn't get enough of each other. Physically or emotionally.

Seri blossomed into a confident, self-reliant woman, who had created an amazing life for herself. I hired her on with my company, and she worked for me while attending university. She majored in accounting and had full intentions of taking over the financing end of the business when I retired. For now, she split her time between my office and her mother's shop.

Her husband, Ivan, was going to stay on as project manager, and I had no doubt they were going to make a great team after I left. I planned to retire this year but hadn't officially done so.

Seri had two boisterous young boys, who were spitting images of Ivan. Waylon was four and Weston was six, and the two were quite the handful. Addie would take them into the garden with her for hours, and they would dig until their hearts were content. A few times they had dug up her daisies, Addie's favourite flowers, but she didn't care. She loved their zest for the outdoors.

When Seri first learned she was pregnant, she was worried she'd pass on her mental illness to her boys, but neither had shown signs of struggles. She kept it in the back of her mind and watched for signs just in case. Ivan had accepted Seri just as she was, and we couldn't have asked for a better son-in-law. Seri shared with him all that had happened in her life, and he was willing to stand by her. She attended therapy every week, and sometimes Ivan went as well to better understand how he could help her when she struggled. For the first few years of their marriage, both Addie and I were worried Ivan might leave when or if Seri hit rock bottom, but he never did. He thought she was the strongest person he had ever met. What many saw as a weakness having OCD, Ivan saw as a strength.

Ivy and Seri became thick as thieves, and Ivy named her first born after Seri and Addie: Seri-Lynn. It took me awhile for the name to flow off my tongue, but I liked it well enough. Addie had cried at the honour. She even jokingly said a speech when she was told Seri-Lynn's name.

"I would like to thank Ivy and Jed for this honour, and to all the little people who stuck by me and knew my name was awesome."

I laughed out loud at the memory. Seri-Lynn was now three, and Ivy was expecting again any day now. Ivy majored in psychology and was a well-respected therapist in town. Although Ivy never said as much, Seri was touched that she chose that profession. Seri was sure it was because of the struggles she lived with.

I heard footsteps on the stairs and stopped fussing with the party arrangements to see who it was. The family was downstairs getting ready. Ivy was the first to reach the top of the stairs, followed by Seri-Lynn and then the boys.

"The troop is ready," said Seri as she entered the kitchen. "Need help carrying anything?"

I nodded and held two bags out for her to grab.

"I'll take the birthday cake," Ivy said. "I don't want anyone dropping the masterpiece I made."

Today was Addie's birthday, and we were celebrating outside in her garden. Jed pushed open the patio doors. It was only a short walk to the spot in the garden where we planned to have our picnic. It was only cake and drinks, but we aimed to make it a memory worth keeping. The family strolled around the planted beds to the bench and table situated near the back of the flower garden. Last year, I had cut down a few trees and helped Addie with landscaping. She wanted a sitting area similar to the courtyard at the hospital. She told me it was in the courtyard where she had found clarity on what her family meant to her and why things happened the way they had. It had also been the place where she had forgiven me. I didn't understand but if she wanted the garden, she was going to get it. She planted a row of shrubs behind the bench that created a wall about 20 feet long and jutted out each side about eight feet.

Flowers of every shade of yellow, orange and red she could imagine grew in front of the shrubs. She had been careful not to choose any that grew more than four feet tall. She wanted to display the shrubbery too. To me, the area was even more beautiful than at the hospital. I figured it was because it was done with her love. The only spot in the garden that Addie hadn't worked on was the hole to the left of the flower bed. I had dug that myself this morning. It was nestled close to the prettiest of rose bushes, one of Addie's favourite flowers.

When everyone had eaten their cake, and the kids had settled, Ivy spoke, emotion weighing heavy in her voice. "I think it's time for a speech, Dad."

Every year I toasted the woman I loved. The woman I had created this wonderful family with. I would do the same this year, and every year for the rest of my life. Once again, it was time. I was unsure of what to say this year. It would be different, not the off-the-cuff remarks I'd usually say. I would start talking and hope I found the right words to share with Addie.

"First, I want to thank everyone for coming today." That was the easy part. From here on out, it was going to be tough. "Next, let me say, Happy Birthday to my best friend, my loving wife, Addie." A lump formed quickly in my throat, and emotions I tried to control were taking over. "You will be pleased to know, we ate your cake right at 6:00 pm. A tradition that still stands."

I turned to face Addie. "Addie, from the day we met in the grocery store, I have never stopped thinking of you. I had seen you around the rink, of course, but that first real conversation with you in the canned food aisle was the day I fell in love with you." Out of the corner of my eye, I saw Seri wiping away a tear.

"We found one another, got lost and then found each other again. Through the good and the bad of our lives, together we managed to raise two beautiful human beings. Well, I like them anyways." Ivy and Seri smiled at me. I returned my gaze to Addie.

"We never gave up on each other. Well, you never gave up on me." The lump clogging my airway dislodged, and I cleared my throat. "You made me a better man by showing me undeserved forgiveness and unconditional love. You put others first, and your love is a gift. Just knowing you changed a person for the better. You taught us all never to be ashamed of who we are, and it's okay to ask for help from others at times in our lives. You made me laugh with your silliness." I almost choked on the irony of the sob caught in my throat as I spoke those words. I fought mightily for composure.

"You made me the happiest man I could have ever asked to be, Addie." I continued to fight the tears that threatened to fall. Wiping the corner of my eye, I pushed on. "I love you so much, and I hope you knew that right up until your last breath." My voice cracked.

I walked to Addie's urn and gingerly picked her up. I kept talking in hopes she could hear me in heaven.

"You put your whole heart and soul into our home. As I look over what you have created, I couldn't imagine laying you to rest any other place but here." I heard sniffling and soft gasps behind me. Stealing a glance at Ivy, I saw her dab her eyes with the back of her hand.

"I promise to visit you every day, Addie. I will love you always." I put two fingers to my lips, kissed them, then touched the urn. "Until we meet again."

The girls wrapped their arms around me and with them at my side, we gently put Addie's ashes in the ground. Dust to dust.

Ivan carefully filled in the hole, and it felt like every shovel full was landing on my heart. I already missed her hand in mine, her lips upon my cheek, her cheerful early-morning smile. My throat tightened, and I fought for breath. I didn't know how I'd live without her. Ivy slipped into my arms and gave me a bear hug to keep me on my feet.

The grandchildren gathered around and were wondering what was happening. They were too young to grasp the concept of their nanny being gone, but the girls felt it important for them to be involved and to understand that when they wanted to be close to Nanny, this was where they could come.

Weston and Waylon missed Addie a lot already, and they were intrigued that they could talk to her at this spot.

"Will Nanny answer me?" Weston asked Seri when she explained what we were doing.

"You will feel her in your heart, Wes. Just like I do." It was Ivy who spoke those words and put a hand to his heart. He hugged his auntie as they cried together. They all stood, unsure of what to do next.

"Can I have a few minutes alone?" I said it quickly, without thought. I needed to be with Addie. See if I could feel her with me.

"Sure, Daddy." Seri quietly led her crew away with Ivy and her family in tow.

I sat on the bench and stared at the freshly turned earth while my thoughts tumbled over one another. How was I going to move forward without Addie by my side? I still couldn't believe she was gone. This morning, I opened my eyes and expected to see her lying in bed beside me. My first thought was she was in the garden, and then reality slammed into my heart, and I cried until I dragged myself from the bed and into the shower. It was cruel that a brain aneurysm had taken her from me on a lovely Friday morning, two days before her fifty-fifth birthday. I took solace in the fact she had died doing what she loved, tinkering in her garden. We had made love that morning, and we were supposed to enjoy the breakfast I had been making after she tended her flowers. She never made it to breakfast.

I looked to the heavens, wondering if she could hear me, tears unabashedly falling from my eyes. I now understood how people died of a broken heart. In time, I would be grateful for every minute God had given me with Addie but right now, I was inconsolable and angry. Why did He have to take her from me so soon?

I closed my eyes and a memory flashed inside my head. I remembered a night we rented a cabin in the mountains, the night I felt we truly reconnected. We were lying together in front of a roaring fire. I could almost feel our embrace, but it was her words I remembered most. She had said that if she was to die that night, she would die a happy woman. She was proud of the resilience our family had shown, and the struggles we went through had only made each day more meaningful to her.

"I thought about taking the easy road," she'd said. "Starting fresh. But you can't have the wonderful moments without the pain. We learn from the harder moments, don't we? I learned I need to see the beauty in times of grief."

I desperately clung to these words of wisdom she'd shared that night. If we hadn't experienced all we had, I likely would never have realized the depth of my love for Addie or experienced such joy. There was peace in knowing she was happy with our life together and a soft reassurance in her words. Life would bring more joys, I was sure, but it was too daunting a task to think of experiencing them without her.

"A sign, Addie. Can you give me a sign that you're still with me?" I swatted at the tears, but it was no use. They kept coming. "I don't think I can go on unless I know you're with me somehow."

At that exact moment, Seri rushed towards me. "Dad! Dad! Come quick. Ivy's water broke." She grinned. "Mom would have loved this. She'd have said it was the perfect birthday gift."

Joy joined the sorrow in my heart. "Thank you," I mouthed silently to the skies.

At 11:42 pm that night, Daisy Adalynn Rose was born.

www.ingramcontent.com/pod-product-compliance
Lightning Source LLC
Chambersburg PA
CBHW020640180626
46816CB00003B/1053